Praise for *Disturbance*

"Told in vivid domestic details flavored by the occult, *Disturbance* embodies the claustrophobic fear and denial that can haunt survivors of abuse long after the danger has passed. This book reads like a poem but hits like a horror novel. What a mysterious, painful, yet strangely delicious slice of life."

—Ashley Hutson, author of *One's Company*

"*When I Hit You* meets *The Craft*—this slim, searing novel lures you in with the delicious nostalgia of teenage witchcraft before breaking you in two with its acute account of emotional and physical abuse. I was left completely breathless."

—Ruth Gilligan, author of *The Butcher's Blessing*

"Jenna Clake's first novel is blazingly emotionally intelligent, caustically well-observed and at times painfully funny. Shot through with the most convincingly uncanny and unsettling latent plot I've encountered in years. Comparisons are odious, but it feels like *Normal People* meets *Twin Peaks*."

—Luke Kennard, author of *The Transition*

"A smart, sinister novel about how an abusive relationship—with its ominous rituals, hexes, and jump-scares—can turn a home into a haunted house. Blood-curdling and bloody brilliant."

—Clare Pollard, author of *Delphi*

"Jenna Clake's sun-baked novel of witchcraft and terrible boyfriends is much more than it seems: a sly and sharply written portrayal of loneliness, the devastating effects of an abusive relationship, and our cultural infatuation with the perceived potential of adolescence. Both bracing and compelling, muted yet blazing with undercurrents of uncanny nostalgia and female rage—a dark and shifty treat."

—Sharlene Teo, author of *Ponti*

"Wonderfully witchy and emotionally astute. *Disturbance* hums with a tense and eerie energy and paints a powerful portrait of a young woman recovering from abuse."

—Chloë Ashby, author of *Wet Paint*

"A hypnotic debut in which a young woman's life becomes intertwined with that of her young neighbor. The narrator's history is delicately unveiled, and I was in awe of the nuanced way in which Jenna Clake handled such a harrowing subject."

—Stacey Thomas, author of *The Revels*

DISTURBANCE

DISTURBANCE

A Novel

Jenna Clake

W. W. NORTON & COMPANY

Celebrating a Century of Independent Publishing

Copyright © 2023 by Jenna Clake
First American Edition 2023

First published in Great Britain in 2023 by Trapeze,
an imprint of The Orion Publishing Group Ltd.

For information about permission to reproduce selections from this book, write to Permissions, W. W. Norton & Company, Inc., 500 Fifth Avenue, New York, NY 10110

For information about special discounts for bulk purchases, please contact W. W. Norton Special Sales at specialsales@wwnorton.com or 800-233-4830

Manufacturing by Lakeside Book Company
Production manager: Louise Mattarelliano

ISBN: 978-1-324-05077-3 (pbk)

W. W. Norton & Company, Inc.
500 Fifth Avenue, New York, N.Y. 10110
www.wwnorton.com

W. W. Norton & Company Ltd.
15 Carlisle Street, London W1D 3BS

1 2 3 4 5 6 7 8 9 0

DISTURBANCE

One

I heard, through my bedroom window, that my neighbours' teenage daughter, Chelsea, was going through a break-up. I looked down onto the front lawn. Chelsea was shouting into her phone that he was a bastard, he didn't love her, and he probably never had. She sounded like she needed someone to wrap their arms around her. She was sat cross-legged on the grass, which was uncut and sprinkled with dandelions, like someone had chewed them and spat them out. The sun flared over the roofs, a July day so hot, the houses across the street shimmered like a mirage.

Our block of flats was made from ugly red brick and had cheap, white windows, the eyesore of an otherwise nice street, which was narrow and lined by refurbished terraced houses, generally occupied by couples and families. Each house had a little raised box for a front garden in which petunias and marigolds wilted, surrendering to the heat.

When the letting agent had met me on the front lawn ten months ago, she'd grinned, 'What do you think?'

'Absolutely fine,' I had said, thinking it looked miserable.

'Great location,' she had said.

We both knew it wasn't true, but it was all I could afford if I didn't want housemates.

I hadn't spoken much to Chelsea's family – the Walkers – who lived in the only other flat in the corridor, or indeed anyone else in the block of flats since I'd moved in ten months before. We nodded and mumbled hellos if we failed to evade each other in the entrance hall or outside our front doors. Most of the time, I rushed up the stairs to my flat as quietly as I could, trying to avoid where the carpet curled like a tongue in case I might trip over. I worried that if I did, the noise of me stumbling would make them come out, and then we'd be forced to talk. After a few questions, I'd inevitably end up telling them that I lived alone, was recovering from a break-up and struggling to do anything.

I daydreamed about my boyfriend a lot, even though I didn't want to. I pictured him staring out of the kitchen window, onto the dark street, the moment before he'd turn around to snarl at me. I couldn't yet refer to him as my 'ex-boyfriend'; it would have felt like he was purged from my life, which he wasn't.

On the front lawn, Chelsea finished her call. She sniffled into the crook of her elbow and began to text. Then she lay down on her back. Wisps of cloud. The grass yellowing, rippling and breathing in the breeze. It stayed light for so long then, the days stretching with possibility, a heat that lingered oppressively, so it was impossible to sleep. Chelsea liked seventies music, like her parents, Liz and Mark, who were in a covers-only band and practised late into the night. She played 'If You Leave Me Now' on her phone, the song tinnily ringing up to my window. Then she switched to Fleetwood Mac. She started crying, quite loudly. She continued to text furiously, the phone held precariously above her face.

She rolled over to lie on her front, then leaned her forehead on her arms. The sun was starting to come down now, leaking a strange purple light over the road. I knew the first few days after a break-up could be difficult – it was all apathy, or hysteria. Lying in bed and crying, or going through everything the person had ever touched and putting it in a black bin bag for a charity shop. It occurred to me that I could have gone down and spoken to her, but I didn't know what to say. I didn't think anyone would appreciate my relationship advice.

I'd seen Chelsea coming and going in her friends' cars. These friends had woken me up a few times at night by driving too fast, or playing dance music loudly with their windows down. I lay awake and listened to them whooshing past, their headlights flashing across the walls, my heart beating faster in response. Chelsea was still having lessons with an elderly instructor who wheezed into the resident's parking spot once a week in his yellow Corsa, which was in constant need of washing. Now that she had finished her A level exams, she sneaked out in the early hours, the communal light in our corridor flickering on, her white trainers glowing as she walked to the end of the road and vanished. I wondered what she was up to – who she could be spending all those hours with. I might have noticed these things, but I also might have made them up. I couldn't be trusted to remember.

From what I could hear with my ear pressed to the cool, paper-thin walls, Chelsea's midnight wanderings meant that she argued with her parents frequently, and her parents then argued with each other after that. A few weeks ago, the Walkers' tempers were fraught; the heat was so furious that one of the neighbours' dogs burnt its paws on the pavement.

Chelsea's mother, Liz, had shouted, 'I would have never been this disrespectful to my parents.'

Chelsea said something back, too muffled for me to catch.

Liz snapped, 'You're grounded.'

Chelsea released a high-pitched yelp. Someone banged a door shut. My plates rattled in the drainer.

'I'm an adult,' Chelsea said. 'And I can't miss prom! *Everyone* is going.'

I'd heard Chelsea slam the Walkers' front door and run down the stairs many times. I was jumpy, not yet used to the flat's idiosyncrasies. There were moments when I thought it was alive, humming with creaks and bangs and scratches, scrapes across the wall in the dead of night when I lay awake, sweating and praying for cool air. I heard someone running above me, even though my flat was on the top floor. I could hear my neighbours flick light switches, and their washing machines rumble and tremble against the laminate. I startled in the middle of the night, panting, yelling, as though someone had grabbed and shaken me. These were oddities I hadn't yet become attuned to but thought I would, eventually, once I had settled in. I'd be lying on the sofa with a handheld fan angled at my face, and the sound of Chelsea's door would make me sit up. It reminded me that there was a real world beyond the building, that Chelsea's life – and mine – extended past its borders.

The Walkers' front door was at a right angle to mine, almost directly next to it. Our flats curved around one another confusingly, so I could hear what they were up to in any room – the metallic ping and scrape of a plug pushed into a socket, someone forcing the vacuum around, thwacking it into the skirting boards – even though I couldn't envisage the layout. I spent much of my time observing the rituals of the Walkers' lives, privately tangling myself in their arguments, following Chelsea's comings and goings, so I felt as if I really knew them, even though we barely spoke.

The Walkers kept their shoe rack outside the front door, which I'd thought was brave when I'd first moved in. I'd had things stolen from outside other flats like this, before I'd lived with my boyfriend: plant pots, parcels, bicycles – once, a doormat. The Walkers were the kind of people who believed that others were fundamentally good: they shared tools and stepladders with our neighbours, with whom they were friends, or offered to water their plants when they went away. This sense of community was something I wanted too, but hadn't yet managed to conjure.

It had taken me two days to find this flat online, sitting in a café, typing in postcodes and trawling through dilapidated garage spaces for rent. I'd moved into the small borough, far away from anyone I knew, with nothing but houses and a high street. The flat had come furnished. The sofa was faux-leather and so old it shed little flakes everywhere. The fridge whined so aggressively at times, I thought it might explode. The person who lived there before me had never cleaned, and I found their little black, curly hairs everywhere, no matter how much I vacuumed and scrubbed. Sometimes, although I couldn't be sure, I was certain that someone had crept in while I was sat facing the wall, frowning at my computer. The cupboard doors would hang open, or I'd walk into the living room to find the sofa cushions flattened, as though someone had been lying across them.

After ten months, all that I'd managed to buy for my flat were two candles with skeletons underneath the wax. One was a human skeleton, the other was a cat. Often, as I watched the wax melt, I'd think about setting fire to the flat and myself, speculating about if there was anything hiding underneath the building's foundations. I was mourning my relationship, and I knew that I'd lost something of myself.

Chelsea was still lying on the grass, plucking the heads off dandelion clocks. She had now stopped sobbing. I went into the kitchen to empty more ice into a glass. I had taken to crunching it, trying to cool down. My kitchen was gloomy, and the cupboards were made of dark wood, so no matter the weather outside, I always needed to switch a light on. This might have explained why I couldn't be bothered to cook much.

Suddenly, channelling through the flat, I heard music – a song played loudly, one that sounded as though it was competing against itself, the bass line in an odd rhythm. I felt called back to my bedroom window. I peered down on the front lawn, with the lights off, hoping I wouldn't be noticed. A red Fiat 500 had pulled up by the front lawn, directly in front of Chelsea, forming a sort of shield from the road. The driver rolled down her window and shifted seats over to the passenger side. She leaned out the window. She was Chelsea's age – dyed black hair in a messy bun, wearing a denim jacket. She had long, fake nails, which she tapped on the edge of the window.

The girl turned the music off, leaving us all suspended in silence. It was almost dark outside now. The weak yellow light of the lamp post made the girls look like they were glowing. Chelsea and the other girl spoke, too quietly for me to hear them. I wanted to know what they were saying, but I was worried that if I opened the windows, they'd hear me.

The dark-haired girl opened her car door and knelt at the edge of the front lawn. She looked around like a cat waiting to pounce, but – I was relieved – not up, where she might have seen me peering. The dark-haired girl brought something out of the pocket of her jacket and placed it on the grass. It looked like a small lump of cloudy ice, and I knew, instantly, that it was important. I felt it was charmed, emitting an energy that sang to me. I thought about some of the possible, plausible objects it could be and came up with two options: a stone or a pebble.

The girl rolled the stone to Chelsea, and the ritual began. The evening's heat was suddenly inflamed, as though it had been summoned; there was a smell of rain, almost sulphuric and bitter. Chelsea leaned forward and cupped the stone in her hand. The girls fell silent, and the smell of rot wafted past me, as though something had crawled to die under my floorboards. My stomach turned, and I held my breath. My fingers tingled, like I'd leaned on my hand for too long.

Chelsea took the stone to her cheek, and started rolling it over her face. The other girl watched her closely, moving her lips rapidly, as if chanting. Chelsea rolled the stone over her face several times, slowly at first, and then with more momentum every time she reached her forehead. Through the darkness, the moon cast white light onto Chelsea and her friend, like it was coming through a magnifying glass. The building had been quiet since the girl had turned off her music. Even the fridge had stopped whining. The road had been empty from the moment Chelsea's friend had arrived. It was as if they and I were the only people in the world; they had cast a spell and everyone else had been put into a trance.

Chelsea returned the stone to her palm. She looked at it for a while, communing with it. The rotten smell passed, and something more pleasant was summoned, a scent unseasonably spring-like: fresh earth, crocuses, daubs of early daisies, the first day it feels safe to sit on grass. Chelsea dug into the ground with her bare hands, and pushed the stone into the soil, and then replaced the grass on top. A chill ran over my arms, the heat unexpectedly broken, as though a breeze had swept through the flat.

The girls tilted their heads upwards to look at the moon, absorbing its light, so their outlines appeared sharper, as if they'd been sculpted. They might have spoken again – their lips moved quickly, not quite in sync. Then, as they dropped their heads, sound flooded back: a siren blared at the end of the road; the Walkers began to tune their guitars; the front gate squeaked; a car tore down the street; my fridge was now louder than before and building to a screech. The noise echoed around my bedroom, like something calling from far away. I stayed where I was, wondering if the girls would hear it and know that I'd been watching them. I felt both inside and outside my body, like I had copied myself and pasted a version slightly over my outline.

The girls shuffled forward on their knees to hug each other. As they held on, the shriek from the fridge slowed and returned to normal. I swallowed, noticing my mouth was dry. When they finally broke apart, Chelsea was smiling. She looked at peace, like every thought had been drained out of her. I wanted to be down there with them, where that feeling – that magic – was possible.

Chelsea gazed out into the middle of the street. The friend was showing her nails, and then pointing to her trainers, like nothing had happened. After a few minutes, Chelsea joined in. She shook her hair loose from her scrunchie and pulled at some strands, as though she was asking the girl's opinion on it. They stayed there for a long time, talking like that. Eventually, Chelsea's friend got up, and went back to the car. She switched her radio on again, but turned the dial down dramatically, so the same clashing song I couldn't name wouldn't pulse into the block. Chelsea waved goodbye and then turned to come inside. I waited by my peephole with my eye pressed to the lens. I touched the walls, moving closer.

She paused outside the Walkers' door. The smell of earth seemed hazy, stronger, like she'd been smoking something. It occurred to me that the whole thing might have been about drugs; I didn't know enough about doing drugs to be sure. I wondered if she could hear me or feel that someone was watching her. I held my breath, but she was just texting again, in the respite before having to go inside. She sighed, then tucked her phone into the pocket of her shorts. She slammed the front door behind her, and the arguing began.

In the early hours of the morning, the block of flats was so quiet, I could hear everything through our flimsy walls: the bathroom tap dripping; someone throwing their glass bottles into the communal bins; a car door being shut down the other end of the road. I had a recurring nightmare that woke me up most nights. I went back to the house I had lived in with my boyfriend, but it was empty and didn't look the same. It was much bigger, labyrinthine, and I ran through corridors it sprouted, into rooms, checking behind the beds and underneath the chests of drawers, looking for something – though I couldn't remember exactly what. In the dream, I tried to be as quiet as possible; I knew I was being haunted by something formless and dark. *Leave me alone*, I shouted at it, scrabbling away, the sound caught in my throat as though blocked. It always ended the same way: I'd stand with my back to the front door, and the presence appeared in the hall. I'd stir before I could see how it was going to harm me, rousing to a bedroom that felt wicked.

Waking up so often in the middle of the night meant that I recognised the sound of the Walkers' door clicking as Chelsea sneaked out. Through my peephole, I saw her shuffling into her trainers. The communal light switched on, so I could see Chelsea clearly, standing on her front doormat. She was in her pyjamas: a grey hoody and a pair of light pink shorts with lace around the bottom. Something wasn't right. She was pale and had dark circles under her eyes. Her face was blotchy, as though she'd been crying or was having an allergic reaction. There was a red mark scored across one of her thighs. She appeared to be waiting for something. Then I realised: she was worried that her parents had heard her. She was listening out for any sign of movement before stealing away.

Suddenly, she darted down the stairs. I moved quickly back through my flat to watch her from the window. We arrived at the same time. Chelsea landed on her knees and tore the grass and mud with her fingers, clumps in her hands like hair. She pulled the stone from the ground, and I expected her to throw it away, because I believed, with shock at my own train of thought, that it must be cursed. The thought felt inevitable, true. My instinct to run to her flared; I wanted to help, to understand what was happening. As I thought this, the centre of my palm stung, as though I were holding the stone. Chelsea took a tissue from her hoody pocket and wrapped the stone up carefully. She cradled it in her hand like an injured bird.

Two beams of white light down the road. Heat rising from the tarmac. She stared at the headlights of the car, which felt so bright I had to shield my eyes. The red Fiat 500 pulled up again, and the dark-haired girl got out. She approached Chelsea carefully, as though she were contagious, and then reached for her elbow, avoiding the stone. She pulled Chelsea towards the car. They drove off, without the radio on, in silence.

Two

The next morning, the birds were singing, and the air was thick and oppressive. It was early, the weak light filtering in, the sky still hazy, yet to be cauterised by the sun. I felt as though something was waiting for me in my bedroom, like I had woken to a spider scuttling across the ceiling. I lay still, trying to steady my breath. I had slept fitfully in the night, taunted by kaleidoscopic images of my recurring dream. I was being chased through the house again. This time, when I found new doors to open, I discovered Chelsea and her friend crouched in the darkness, chanting, murmuring to one another. They turned to look at me, then disappeared. I carried on running.

As I rolled over to face the window, trying to come round, I heard chafing, like nails raked against wood. The noise was persistent, someone scratching an insatiable itch. Then, as though someone had turned off a machine, the sound stopped. When I tried to turn on my lamp, the light bulb fizzled and sputtered, then died. I hid under the thin sheet, damp with sweat, frightened to face the world.

Eventually, I climbed out of bed and opened the blinds,

trying to steady my heartbeat. I wondered if I had imagined the disruption, believing I was awake when I was in fact dreaming. I was determined to make myself feel normal, and told myself that if the street outside looked ordinary, then everything would be fine. The leaves on the trees shone, light filtering through, mottling my bedroom walls. I wondered if summer would ever end, and felt panicked by its crawl. I looked up, into the cloudy glare of the sun, and whispered to the world: *Show me a way out.*

My mind kept on returning to Chelsea and her friend. In my dream, they hadn't been surprised to see me. They had regarded me with a sort of cool inevitability, as though they had been expecting me to throw open the door and find them. They had been leaning over something conspiratorially, whispering secrets to one another – another spell, I supposed, if I could trust that line of thought. What was the stone they'd passed between them? Through my peephole, Chelsea had looked frightened, afraid of what was happening to her. I hadn't heard her come back.

I did the most obvious thing: I googled Chelsea. I found her Instagram profile easily, which surprised me, because her full name wasn't uncommon. I knew it had something to do with algorithms, but I didn't know exactly how that worked. I had an old Instagram account that I'd wiped clean after leaving my boyfriend and hadn't bothered to start over again. I logged in, hoping that I wouldn't be confronted by anything from my old life, and was relieved by the blank space when my account loaded.

In her profile photo, Chelsea had one foot in front of the other to make her legs appear slimmer, posing her body at an angle. She was wearing a short, light blue crêpe dress and had a tiny black handbag in her hand. Her other hand was pushed into her waist, obviously intended to accentuate it. It was also the latest photo on her grid, taken three weeks ago. I scrolled down. There was a series of similar images; the captions were always emojis. Chelsea didn't willingly reveal much of her real life. If there had been photos of her boyfriend on her profile before, there weren't any now. Everything was artfully crafted, an impression of a life that felt almost familiar and convincing, but omitted everything important.

Later, at my computer, I scrolled back as far as I could, ignoring the ping of emails flooding my inbox, trying to find any sign of the magic I'd witnessed: crystals, talismans, black lace, skulls – the things I foolishly considered hall-marks of their craft. I needed to know more about Chelsea, and her friend, and what they were doing. I had questions now, something more than spreadsheets and team meetings to think about.

I clicked a username, and then Jess appeared. Her grid was also curated to give nothing about her real life away. In one photo, she was on a blue bike, facing away from the photog-rapher, down a wide path lined by trees about to become bare, the last few orange leaves burning in the distance. The caption: *Summer is over and I'm not okay with that.*

Chelsea and Jess didn't even post photos of food – which was something everyone did, no matter their age – as if they had transcended their bodily needs. No one, not even the people who knew them, would know they had done mysterious things with a stone in the middle of the night. There wasn't the slightest sense of disturbance.

I spent the whole morning scrolling, then googling (*stone + magic, stone + spell*). My searches directed me to websites selling magic stones, gravelly lumps which could banish negative energy and transform pessimistic thoughts into optimistic ones. One of the descriptions added: *UV light needed to see magic.*

Then I found spells. I learned that it was possible to cast a love charm with a stone, but it required deep fixation on a specific kind of crystal and staring at photos of the 'target' during the full moon. On a witch's blog, I read about creating a love spell with imagination alone, no objects required. But this wasn't what I was looking for; I moved on. Finally, I found something that resembled what Chelsea and Jess had been doing. The spell could be cast to banish negative energy. In the description of this specific 'protection spell', an egg was used, supposedly symbolising a new life after the end of something bad. It didn't have to be used for a break-up, but it was often used in this way. *Especially useful for ending negative connections*, the description stated.

When I'd first moved into the flat, there had been different boys coming to pick Chelsea up each weekend – a black Mini, a silver Golf, a blue BMX she'd sit on the handlebars of – until she whittled it down to the one who became her boyfriend. Joseph – a name I'd learned through the walls – was tall and wore different trainers every time he visited. I'd overheard their arguments. They'd stand out on the front lawn, Joseph's feet planted widely. He often put his hands into his pockets.

Once, he'd said, 'Who are you going with?'

'What?' Chelsea said.

'Is it going to be safe?'

'Of course it's going to be safe.'

'Who's going to be there?'

'I don't know. People. Do you want me to write a list?'

'Don't lie to me. I deserve to know.'

There was a lot of shouting when Joseph was around, but he and Chelsea would still end their meet-ups with long kisses and promises of love. As things went on, he always seemed to be at the Walkers' flat, or out the front of the building. If Joseph behaved this way in public, admonishing Chelsea, calling her names, I could only imagine what he'd do when no one was watching. I knew from experience that the accusations could only worsen, and then something terrible would happen. Sometimes, Joseph would roll down the window of his black Fiesta to shout *I love you* at Chelsea as he drove away, and I felt a pang, like I was being dragged back in time to watch my errors, and I should warn Chelsea of the consequences.

Chelsea still hadn't returned to the Walkers' flat, and I began to worry that she'd become lost, disorientated by whatever she and Jess had done the night before. I realised, suddenly, that I was hungry. The fridge was empty, which meant I needed to go to the shop, which also meant I could keep an eye out for Chelsea. I usually left my flat for two things. The first was to pick up something to eat every few days − a loaf of bread, instant noodles, a microwave lasagne that I could make last several meals, a bag of salad. The second was to go on a walk. My ritual: out onto the main street, past the pub and the sickly yellow petrol station, which was unfailingly empty, to the park. Inside the pub, the chairs were stacked on top of the table, abandoned for the patios out the back. If the weather was nice, I tried to meander for longer to avoid being in the flat for as long as possible, the clunks and bangs oppressive when I'd spent too much time there.

As I got into the shower, groggy and unclean, I heard Alice and Sean having sex. They lived directly beneath me, so I heard them three times a week, on a Tuesday, Friday and Saturday. It was Saturday afternoon. When I had first moved in, I could hear them fucking constantly, every day, but as the months had gone on, they had developed their routine. I could hear Alice and Sean most clearly from the bathroom, their moans and giggles and sneezes echoing through the wall, as though they lived with me.

I heard all of this because I worked from home as Head of Operations for a small energy company. After I'd moved into the flat, I'd found the job easily, as though someone had summoned it for me. Just as I'd begun to feel settled into my new role, my office had been closed – part of a nationwide trend to save money. My work usually involved ordering gas and electricity supplies and managing the switch of suppliers for new customers. On the best days – the only days of work that I enjoyed – I'd get lost for hours trying to resolve mixed-up meters on the national database. It was logical and unemotional. It kept my mind off my boyfriend, and with too much work to do, and not enough staff, I would often work into the night and then collapse on my bed in the early hours of the morning when I couldn't keep my eyes open. I kept strange time, which meant I hadn't made many new friends and saw and heard things of which most other people would be ignorant.

When I made my way to the front door, Alice came out of her flat and stopped me. She had a shiny, dark brown bob which she tucked behind her ears, then flicked out girlishly. She stood on her mat in her socks, wearing a pair of Sean's boxers and one of his old T-shirts. I felt a lump in my throat, which I tried to swallow. Alice and I hadn't talked much, because talking to her was demoralising. She had everything I'd once possessed, or everything I could have had, and standing in front of her made me feel like tipping my head back and wailing.

'I have some sad news!' said Alice. 'We've bought a Victorian terrace not far away. We're going to be moving in about six weeks, if the decorators *actually* do their jobs.'

'That's great,' I said. 'Really great.'

'Don't worry! We can't bear to live in it while it's being sorted out – so much work! We'll be around a while longer. I personally think Sean is reluctant to leave the flat, so I'm trying to win him over. He just really doesn't like change.'

I pulled at a piece of skin at the base of my nail. It sliced deeply, and blood prickled to the surface. I stuck my finger in my mouth.

'I mean, I know it's a cliché,' she said, tucking her hair behind her ears. 'But we've started an Instagram account for the renovation.'

'Oh,' I said, around my finger.

'All the good usernames were taken,' she said, flicking her hair back out. 'We ended up with one with lots of underscores. I hate that, it seems so infantile.'

'Me too.'

'But it's just for fun!'

She showed me the account on her phone. The handle was *our_little_victorian_terrace_alice_and_sean*, which was too long, but I didn't say anything. They had slightly over two hundred followers already, which, Alice admitted, were mostly other Victorian terrace renovation accounts. The house was going to have a colour palette of grey. She had taken photos of the light streaming through the windows, and folded grey towels which had been monogrammed. Sean was always being referred to in the captions, so it was clear that Alice was the narrator.

'We bought so much!' she said. 'We *promised* we wouldn't buy things, because it was so much more important to get the carpets done. And the painting. But I couldn't help myself. Sean spent all day yesterday choosing a shade for his man cave – don't worry, it's *ironic* – so I just needed something else for myself.'

'I know what you mean,' I said, trying to smile. I wiped my finger against my jeans.

I had seen little of Sean. He was short, had a beard, and grunted if I passed him in the hallway. Of the two, Alice was more friendly. I sometimes smelt yeast coming from their flat, late into the night, which made me think Sean was obsessively baking bread. Alice hadn't ever said anything, though.

'We'll miss this place,' said Alice. 'We just really want a garden.'

'Yeah, plants are really nice. Good for the air or something, I heard.'

'And it's too noisy here, don't you think?'

'Hm, sometimes,' I said. 'Did you hear that noise the other night? It was like someone sawing metal.'

'I don't think so,' said Alice. She paused to think. 'But, anyway, if you get any boxes from deliveries, will you save them for us?'

'I'll try,' I said. 'But you can buy them, probably online, flat-packed.'

'No,' said Alice, shaking her head furiously, like I'd said something offensive.

There was an awkward pause before Alice started talking again.

'We're getting a dog. Sean wants a Labrador, but I want a Pomeranian. Don't you think a Pomeranian would be cute? We're going to call it Piglet.'

Begrudgingly, I admitted that I thought it was a good name. Then Alice said Sean was calling her from inside the flat, but I didn't hear him.

'Honestly, he can't even make a bacon sandwich.' She rolled her eyes dramatically, and then disappeared back inside.

My forehead felt sweaty. As I pulled open the door to the block, the sun slid behind a cloud. I was grateful for the cool air. I decided to walk to the park and then on my way back I'd go to the shop. Each time I thought of eating something, I imagined it sliding down and straight out my body, turning to nothing. I ate bland things when I could manage, and even then, whatever I had eaten felt like it was poking at my ribs, eager to get out.

As I walked, the world was too loud. Sirens, cars accelerating to beat the traffic lights, people talking obnoxiously.

It felt like someone had rubbed an old, damp cloth over everything. The sky was thick with cloud now, threatening humid rain, washing it all out into a dull blueish tint. Then, the sudden quiet of the empty park – an expanse of grass surrounded by trees, on an incline. If I stood at the bottom, all I could see was grass, or patches of mud where someone had slipped trying to walk up. If I stood at the top, right in the middle, I could see the whole space and everyone in it. From there, I could look at all the expensive, detached houses surrounding it. I listened to the birds rustling in the trees, the stillness of the houses, and tried to feel calm.

The grass was damp under my feet, and slippery. When I got to the top of the hill, people began to turn the lights on in their houses. Kitchen and bedroom windows lit up, one by one in a string, emitting a dark orange glow. The air was perfectly still. I walked around the perimeter three times, pausing at the top. I looked down at the houses, which appeared to be frozen: no one came in or out, or moved across the windows.

Then Chelsea and her friend, Jess, entered the park. I was surprised and relieved to see them – Chelsea was safe. Jess came in first, a full tote bag on each shoulder. Chelsea lagged behind, still in her pyjamas and trainers, looking dazed.

'Nearly there,' called Jess, impatiently. She moved ahead, tucking herself into one of the trees at the crest of the hill.

I took a few steps back and hid in the shadows, watching. They wouldn't see me if I kept quiet. The wind picked up in the trees; the branches shivered. I could no longer see the sky. The conifers sounded like they were whispering and then shushing one another for speaking too loudly.

Jess pulled out candles and lit them with a cigarette lighter. She arranged them in a circle. The candles were thick and creamy white. The flames flickered, but the wicks managed to stay lit. Jess growled as the lighter burned her thumb, shaking her hand as if to put it out. The animal noise carried up the hill and into my ear.

Chelsea finally joined her. She flopped down onto the grass and sat cross-legged. She rubbed her hands over her face, pushing her palms into her eye sockets. The air was a bonfire: earthy, deep, the kind of smell I knew would cling to my hair and stay there for days.

Jess prised open Chelsea's hand, forcing a candle into her palm. She folded her own hand over Chelsea's, so that they both clasped the stem. This time, they placed it down on the grass and left it to burn. As a gust of wind blew through the trees, the whisper of the branches sounded like a crowd. Smoke curled around me, and needles prickled across my hands again.

I felt drawn towards them, called down the hill to their coven, charmed by the smoke and their secret. I had settled on the theory that Chelsea, with the help of Jess, had poured all her bad feelings about Joseph, and their break-up, into the stone. When she rolled it across her face, she had asked it to take those bad feelings from her; she had wanted to banish Joseph. But their spell had been jinxed, flawed, and so now the stone was torturing Chelsea. On the websites I'd been reading, there were many warnings against getting a spell wrong; there could be disastrous consequences.

Jess took the stone and placed it into Chelsea's hand and then helped her up from the grass. They said something urgently, lips moving in a litany. Chelsea crawled to the roots of a tree and reached her arm down through the earth to bury the stone. As she pushed the soil back, covering the hole, the air cooled. Chelsea stared at the ground.

As though the clouds had been sliced open, rain began to fall in a deluge, thundering through the trees. Beneath my feet, the grass grew dense and boggy.

'Come on,' said Jess, pulling Chelsea up. 'It's happening. We should get out of here.'

Their hair clung to their faces, sodden in seconds. The rain pounded into the ground, and puddles sprouted across the park; my clothes were saturated and stuck to my skin. Jess seemed eager to leave, glancing around, as though someone was coming for them. I held my breath and my feet sank further into the grass. My socks were completely soaked through. Jess started packing the candles into the tote bags, almost throwing them, and barking orders at Chelsea.

The girls ran down the hill and out of the park, shouting about the rain, Chelsea trailing behind Jess. I waited, then left my hiding place as slowly and quietly as I could, frightened of what I might unleash if I suddenly revealed myself. I had to be sure that my theories were correct; I had to be certain I knew what they were up to.

I crouched by the patch where they had been digging: a small mound of upturned grass among the roots, but no one else would have noticed. I reached my hand down beneath the roots of the tree and found the stone. It was smooth and warm, like it had been boiled and left to cool. As I cupped it, I felt it pulse with the heat of Chelsea's pain, and I knew I was right.

Three

It occurred to me that my boyfriend was abusive about a year before I left him. When he was out at work, I called in sick and got back into bed, hiding under the duvet where I didn't feel so evil. Under the duvet, it didn't matter what I'd done. I felt the sun warm the sheets, and imagined I was being absolved for the shouting, the crying, the things I had said, whatever I had done to provoke him. One day, as I was lying there, I had followed an impulse and googled his behaviour. This soon became something I did almost every day. Each time, I was directed to women's refuge websites and pages about domestic abuse. I would close the tab, then reopen it to check if the signs were the same, or if I'd misread them, or they'd been updated.

When one website said, *If you're googling your partner's behaviour, then something is wrong*, I thought: *Okay*. But I could see why my boyfriend was angry with me, so it didn't seem so bad. I was annoying, a bit overbearing. I was a morning person, and he wasn't. He didn't like anchovies, and I did. I didn't have many of my own friends left, and at that time, my boyfriend was staying out later; I was unbearable to be around, he said. He'd come home drunk and swear at me, or fall asleep on the train, and then say it was my fault when he had to get a taxi home. Sometimes, he wouldn't come back at all, and I wondered if something awful had happened. I'd text and call, waiting for him, and then he'd come back at the end of the day, oblivious, and ask what I'd made for dinner. He'd tell me to relax around him, that I could be myself, and then I'd make a joke about sex, which he found disgusting. I could see that he'd been very generous in loving me. I hadn't given him enough time to himself, or spent too much time on my own. I had no sense of how to keep him happy, making blunders even when I knew what his facial expressions or silences meant. I just always did things wrong, and that must have been frustrating. Sometimes I thought: *Yeah, I'd throw me across the landing, too.*

When I'd met my boyfriend, I had been careful. Back then, I went out every Friday and Saturday, my calendar fizzing with places to go. We'd been introduced by mutual friends at several house parties. We were acquaintances who sometimes recalled details from each other's lives. He'd worked for the government, I remembered. Something enigmatic. 'How are the secret missions treating you,' I asked him. ('Any honey traps lately?' when I'd had a few too many drinks.) I knew it was dangerous to get entangled with a mutual friend. The concerned, self-interested whispers about how it was going; the phone calls and text messages when things went off the rails; running into him with someone else, inevitably. I liked my life to be quiet, uncomplicated.

I had been single my entire life, save a few melodramatic flings. So, I knew that dating a friend of a friend meant complications: there were preconceptions, expectations, since we 'knew' each other, and I felt people watching over our shoulders. At each party, he offered to help me with things, or introduce me to people he knew and I might like, and so I took his number, and never called, worrying he was just being polite.

It really began, though, at a Christmas get-together. I was waiting for a taxi outside the pub, and he'd come to give me some company. I didn't remember us talking that night — there had been shots, and the women had mostly been squashed on the dance floor while the men drank in their seats — but there he was, in jeans and a shirt, unbothered by the sleet which clung to my hair. I shivered, hugging one arm around myself as we walked up and down the taxi rank, the soles of my feet throbbing. And then, when no one else would take me home, and he'd offered to walk me, I'd turned to him and said, *We should get a drink sometime.*

At first, we'd kept things casual, meeting in a café by my office after work. *Can you find somewhere we won't be disturbed?* he texted. He said he too was a private person. He had many friends in the city, and he didn't want to run into them, because he wanted to give me all his attention. I had my doubts about this — what was he concealing, or who was he hiding me from? But I also knew the misfortune of walking around the city, feeling anonymous, only to run into a friend — my hair greasy, my face pale, my clothes old and worn. I made pointed jokes about hiding in plain sight, and laughed at how he really was a spy now. When we were together, I often left half my coffee, afraid to pick it up in case I spilled it.

Then, a few dates in, after I had cooked him dinner at my flat, we migrated into a loose pattern: he came over and fucked me, and stayed the night, or left – it was hard to predict. Sometimes he brought a takeaway with him. I remember not eating properly, picking at things with a fork, being too fraught with excitement of what I hoped was growing between us, the dread of waiting to see if he'd text again.

He made up his mind after six weeks, abruptly and inexplicably, and willed our relationship into being, insisting we went for dinners in restaurants with white tablecloths. And I was happy to oblige, baffled and pleased by his sudden commitment, his unexpected enthusiasm. When we knew each other better, two months in: a hidden Indian restaurant with two tables, a Japanese restaurant with TVs playing in the background. Me, always pushing the food around my plate, drinking quickly so I'd be charming and funny for him. One evening, three months after our first date, over a candle which nearly burned my wrist, he gave me a key to his house. Glinting, with a little orange tag.

Despite my giddiness, my hope that this might be something promising, something stable and worth exposing myself for – I had never been lucky enough to find something serious – I thought things might be moving too quickly. I woke up and went to sleep feeling like the relationship was happening around me, that I had no control over the way things were developing, or how I moved through them. There was something buzzing inside me. I couldn't sit still, and shook my leg if I was in a meeting or at my desk. My teeth chattered. I was certain I was coming down with something; I felt constantly nauseated, feverish. I walked everywhere, hoping to burn the feeling away.

Another night at the pub, we announced that we were an official couple by arriving together. Our friends threw their arms around us, saying we were perfect for one another. They'd thought it all along. Later, when we had drunk too much, the women turned to me.

'You're not going to hurt him, are you?' someone said. 'Because he's such a lovely person. I'll kill you if you do anything to him.'

The women's laughter rippled around the table.

'No, I'd never do that. I'm not like that at all,' I said.

When I told my housemate I was moving out, he stuck his head into the fridge and said, 'Sure, fine, as long as you find someone to replace you.'

A man who liked video games took my room, and stuck posters of half-naked female characters to the walls before I'd officially left. As I packed my things into boxes and carrier bags, I thought, *Too soon*, and I replied to myself, too quickly, as I would come to learn, *You can always leave.*

For a while, I had liked my boyfriend's house, especially when I was alone. It had its own small yard to grow things, excellent transport links. I could meet my friends at our favourite pub in less than twenty minutes, if I caught the right train. The neighbours included young families, couples just married, everyone heading to the station in the morning or driving off to work. I couldn't believe he'd been living somewhere so idyllic, and felt he'd been waiting to find the right person – me – to share it with. So I didn't mind that his furniture didn't match, or that things were a little old. I thought it was charming, at least.

But as things got worse, and I was left in the house alone for longer periods, I knew that the rooms weren't really my own, that they weren't decorated the way I wanted. I worried that someone might notice, somehow, in the way the books were arranged, or the cracks in the tiles in the bathroom, how everything was completely wrong. My belongings were suddenly gauche and exposing. I realised that I didn't have a sense of style, that I didn't know how to put things together. It was like a light had been switched on, or a lens had been removed, and I could see what had been lurking beneath.

Not long after we had moved in together, less than a week, in fact, he came home in the early hours of the morning, panting as though he'd been running from something dreadful.

'Where have you been?' I said.

He ignored me, stumbling across the bedroom into the chest of drawers, pulling one with such force, it came out completely and smashed onto the carpet.

'Stop, stop,' I called, coming towards him. 'Let me help.'

I had my arms outstretched, my plan to comfort him, to prevent further destruction. To embrace him, put him to bed. I knew not to approach an animal like this, with no warning, but no one had ever explained boyfriends to me.

'Fuck off,' he said as he lashed out towards me, connecting solidly with my arm.

The bruise appeared instantly – angry, red. It would take weeks to go down.

I screamed, and ran onto the landing, crying.

'You hit me, you hit me, you hit me,' I said, sitting down on the top step, when I should have been moving towards the door.

The situation felt unreal, nightmarish, as though I would wake up any moment and curl towards my boyfriend's sleeping body, instinctively looking for protection.

He was remorseful that time. He followed me and put his arms around me. I decided not to recoil. He buried his head into my shoulder and cried too, harder than I did. I took that as proof that he hadn't meant it.

'You shouldn't have done that,' he said.

The next day, I called my mum from the car. It was dark outside, the office lights streaming out onto the car park. I'd stayed at work late to avoid him, finding the idea of returning to the house unbearable, busying myself with trivial administrative tasks, like cleaning out my desk. When the distractions failed, I sneaked off to the toilets to check and touch the bruise on my arm.

'He hit me,' I said.

'What are you going to do?' my mum asked.

'I'm sure it was an accident,' I said, uncertain if I was lying to her. 'But I'm not very pleased about it. He said he was sorry – or I know he was, anyway.'

My mum paused. I heard her breathing steadily down the phone. 'He shouldn't have done that to you.'

'I think he was just drunk,' I offered. 'He didn't mean it. He was probably just confused.'

My mother said my name slowly.

'I don't want it to be awkward. Please don't say anything when you see him.'

'We just want you to be happy,' she said.

'Yeah,' I said.

'You can always come back home.'

When I hung up, the lights in the office had been switched off. I turned the key in the car's ignition, and forced myself to pull out of the car park. Raindrops ran down the windscreen, obliterating themselves as they crashed into one another.

In the first month after breaking up with my boyfriend, I moved into the flat, got the new job and became a stereotype: went to all-women's exercise classes; stopped eating; called my mother daily, asking, *When will this feel better?* (*No one goes through life unscathed*, she said.) Even though I was living somewhere new, I fretted about running into him, in train stations, on escalators, in the supermarket, holding a frozen pizza, having been crying, or looking exhausted or ill. I walked everywhere quickly and avoided anywhere I thought he might be. I felt that he might be hiding behind shelves in shops, waiting for me on the other side of a zebra crossing, or driving any car that slowed down as it went by. I felt the streets conspiring against me. I thought all the car headlights were being directed onto me, illuminating my shame.

My eyes were sunken and my skin dry and flaking. I'd bitten my nails so much, I'd got infections. I didn't want him to see me like that, to see that I'd become disgusting without him. I considered chopping my long hair to a chin-length bob. I worried that if I saw him and I hadn't changed my hair, he would think that I had stagnated, that I wanted him back. If I cut it, he would think I was trying to be someone else. I had the haircut, then realised my error, and dedicated myself to growing it again, so that it now hung, unkempt, at my shoulders. I worried that other people might see my new style and think that I was sad, jealous or tragic. Whatever I did, I was the trope of a heartbroken woman.

My workplace offered six free sessions of counselling, so I referred myself in March, half a year after I'd joined, after I'd moved. I met my counsellor in a building with rent-by-the-hour office spaces. I walked from my office to the sessions every week with dread. The entrance to the building was down a side street filled with industrial bins and, sometimes, other people smoking, waiting for their own counselling sessions.

My counsellor was a middle-aged woman named Audrey, who wore bright red costume jewellery. We sat on our too-small tub chairs and tried to pretend the space was relaxing. I skirted around the true issue; we spoke about my stress levels at work instead and what I was doing in my free time to make myself feel better.

'I feel like weekends are pointless,' I said. 'I don't know what to do with myself.'

Audrey liked when I uttered these sorts of statements. She could then deliver one of her self-proclaimed 'nuggets of insight'.

'You're allowed to have a bad weekend, you know,' said Audrey.

'Oh, you're right. I'd never thought of it like that,' I said.

It was true, I hadn't ever thought about it, but it was hardly an epiphany.

We did some work on building my self-esteem, which amounted to saying 'no' a bit more at work ('Remember that *No* is a complete sentence,' said Audrey, looking pleased with herself). I knew that six sessions of therapy wouldn't be sufficient to work through everything I felt about my boyfriend – and thereby myself – after four years of being with him. I believed that I couldn't open that up; it would take years to recover, and I couldn't afford a private therapist. I knew that if I really started, I'd probably never leave therapy, depleting any financial security I might claw back for myself. At the end of the sessions, I thanked Audrey and told her she'd really changed things for me. I even bought her a card, which made me feel terrible. I was such a liar.

One thing she'd taught me to do when I was stressed was distract myself, so I tried to stop the thoughts about my boyfriend by humming or saying something out loud to break the spell. Mostly, though, I ended up saying my own name over and over, like I was calling myself back to the real world.

Four

The morning after seeing Chelsea in the park, I had several texts from Eddie. I knew Eddie from my office, before it had been shut. He worked in the finance department. He wore band T-shirts and skinny jeans, and gave the impression of being in his early twenties, even though he was slightly older than me, and owned his own flat. Every month, Eddie would diligently text and see if I wanted to meet him for a coffee, or a drink, or a walk, and I'd run through excuses in my mind until I capitulated and said yes.

He refused to write in paragraphs and sent one sentence at a time, ten messages where one would have sufficed. Sometimes he only sent one word. I hadn't heard from him in a while, but he hadn't said anything important.

Eddie: *Sorry if that was a bit much*
I have a lot to say
Let me know if you want to meet up

It's not that I didn't like Eddie. I was just nervous to be friends with someone. I'd lost a lot of friends in the break-up.

It had been a necessary part of moving away. Shortly after, travelling back to the flat after I'd been visiting my parents, I'd passed a mutual friend at the entrance to the train station. I stopped to say hello, and waved. It was raining, the kind like mist, which seemed to hang, unmoving, and made an umbrella useless. The friend had deliberately looked away, pulling his hat further down his face, and pretended to be lost in the crowd. I'd watched him walk down the ramp to the train station, knowing then that my boyfriend had won. He would disparage me to anyone who would listen, creating some story of my insanity, *my* cruelty. Our relationship had always been a series of games, a frustrating kiss-chase where he tripped me over as I finally reached him. I'd always been the loser.

But there were other friends, ones I'd had before my boyfriend, or ones who I'd thought of as being my friends, really, who hadn't been in touch. I'd made excuses at first – it was a busy time, or perhaps they had their own personal things happening, so they couldn't face the drama of a break-up. Perhaps they thought we'd get back together, or they were waiting for me to sort myself out before being in contact again. Then, when I'd reached out, and heard nothing in return, and I'd realised no one was going to contact me, I changed my number and made a new email address.

The first time I'd met Eddie for coffee, I'd assumed he wanted to talk about work, but he spent a lot of time asking me about myself. I'd tried not to answer these questions too personally, in case he thought we were on a date. He didn't need much prompting to talk about himself. Eddie said that he looked after his elderly mother quite a lot and that meant he'd struggled to make friends when he moved here – most of his evenings and weekends were spent with her. He thought that I might be struggling to meet people too. It was a small town. I said, yes, I hadn't even figured out the bus system yet and didn't know who to ask. That made Eddie assume we were alike. He decided we were friends before I even had a chance to say anything about it.

I often felt exhausted by the prospect of meeting him, apprehensive, perhaps because we hadn't yet settled into one another. But at the end of every coffee, I told myself that I hadn't been too awkward or strange. One thing I liked about Eddie was that he didn't try to touch me. He didn't try to hug me, and he never even put his hand on my arm to draw my attention to things when we were walking around, which was often a subtle sign of someone hoping to get closer.

There had been an incident, the previous December. The office had officially closed in November, and Eddie said he was bored – wasn't I? We'd gone to an indoor market, me following him around as he pointed out rare records, odd little trinkets, second-hand books he thought I might like. The wind tunnelled through the market, so that everyone inside – milling around the shops, sitting on the stools by the restaurants and bakeries – squinted against it. Eddie had spent a long time chatting to a shopkeeper about the weather – *so cold, much colder than last year* – and bought several bags of discounted bananas, grapes, apples and kiwis. When I'd asked him what he was going to do with them all, he'd suddenly looked sad and said, *I don't really know.*

The bags were too heavy for him to carry alone, so we'd caught the bus to his flat.

He'd shown me around, while I sipped a cup of tea, trying to warm myself. I was tired, especially moving from the cold into the warmth. The thought of going back outside was unappealing, and so I let myself relax a bit. The flat was nice, if a little cluttered. There was something on every surface, nowhere to put anything down.

'How's the tea?' he said, awkwardly.

'Honey,' I said, after a sip.

'Sorry?'

'In the camomile,' I said.

'I hope you don't mind,' he said, looking intently at his mug.

'It's great.'

We hovered in the living room. Eddie was overexcited, picking things up and showing them to me like a child who hasn't seen someone new in a while. He pulled a yellow blanket from the sofa. The blanket was thinly knitted like a shawl. He draped it over his arms like a damsel.

'I got this at the shop by the bus stop,' he said. 'The one with the pumpkins in the window? Next to the florist?'

'Oh!' I said, pleased with myself. 'I've been there. I bought some candles. They have skeletons inside them.'

'Yeah, it's cool. The people who run it are really nice, they moved here to *escape the city.*'

'I used to like living in a city,' I said. 'It's a bit odd here, isn't it? Sort of a town, but too big to know anyone, really. Ages anyway from anything major.'

'When most people move here, they want the illusion of being cut off from things,' Eddie said. 'They think it will be peaceful and quiet, and then realise there's little to do. Everyone sort of wants to escape the city eventually, even if they do love it. But they don't want to move *too* far away either.' He looked away. 'I didn't mean that about you.'

Most of Eddie's sentences were inflected slightly upwards at the end; a lot of what he said sounded like a question, so that I felt encouraged to say more.

'I like it here,' I lied. 'Sometimes I felt it was – the city, I mean – just this gallery of memories. Like, *oh I've been there with so-and-so*, or *here is where that thing happened*. So I think it's easy to want to skirt past it all, or find something new. Like, I found that I was avoiding specific routes, until it was taking me twice as long to get anywhere. I think it's easy for people to convince themselves that the problem is the place.'

'What was the problem for you?' asked Eddie.

'I realised I had backed myself into a corner,' I replied, answering evasively, lightly. 'It was a series of things, I suppose. Then I got the new job, which wasn't really worth moving for, now I think about it.'

'Don't you miss it, though?' he said.

I thought about it: bumping into friends on my lunch break; a spontaneous drink after work in a new bar; the doughnut shop with an exceptional playlist. I imagined my boyfriend attached to me at the sleeve, jerking my arm down or back, painfully. I'd felt like I was constantly holding my breath.

'I don't know,' I said. 'Probably not.'

Eddie inhaled loudly, gasping to change the conversation.

'This is honestly the softest thing ever,' he said.

I didn't see what was coming. Before I knew it, he crossed the living room and put the blanket up against my cheek. I flinched, and electricity sparked against my skin – the kind that hurt, shocked. Eddie recoiled. Perhaps he had intended to close the space between us – perhaps I had given off something I hadn't meant to. I waited for him to explode, to rebuke me, to accuse me of being a bitch. With my boyfriend, any gesture or mistake was enlarged and pulled apart, until it was clear I had intended to harm him. The silence hung like a web.

I tried to laugh, but it had sounded tinny and weak. The living room suddenly felt barren and draughty. A patch bloomed into a blush on Eddie's cheek, like I'd struck him. Conditioned by my boyfriend, I felt humiliated by my inability to control myself. My body, so unruly, always projecting my emotions outwards, onto others. My boyfriend said I was unable to hide my bad moods, my indiscretions; they had a smell; they wafted around the house.

'Sorry,' I said after a few moments. 'Living alone, you know.'

'Ow,' he said, laughing. 'That hurt. Did you charge yourself today or something?'

'Battery's running low,' I said. 'I get sparky in the afternoon.'

'Your hair *is* a bit staticky.'

We laughed then, and sat on opposite sides of the room: him stretched out across the sofa, me perched on the armchair, gazing out at the hail that had just begun to bounce along the street.

★

I texted Eddie back, arranging to meet him in the afternoon. I was reluctant to leave the flat and miss Chelsea's comings and goings, looking for a sign of what the spell had done, but I knew I should say yes – it had been a while, and the flat was stifling, suffocated by a heatwave that my news app reported was going to break records. I'd checked Chelsea's Instagram account, willing it to show me something new, but she hadn't updated it. Jess's profile was similarly frozen, no matter how often I refreshed.

I was late, on account of my scrolling, and rushed through the town, almost bumping into people slurping at ice creams. The town had a few cafés, but only one that was acceptable, housed above a bike shop. There was pine furniture, white walls and chalkboards instead of menus. Plants hung from the ceiling, as though poised to fall on someone's head. Eddie had chosen to sit on one of the wooden benches by the window, which looked out onto the street. He waved at me. A few people were typing on their laptops, but, mostly, the café was occupied by couples having late lunch, sheltering from the sun, trying to finish their iced coffees before they melted. I felt like I saw happy couples wherever I went – arms around one another, smiling blissfully – even though I knew that couldn't be true. I tried not to pay them any attention.

I slid across the bench to sit as close to the window as possible. Eddie had already ordered for me. I felt myself growing drowsy in the stream of light coming through the glass. My hands were sweating.

As soon as I asked him how he was, Eddie launched into a lengthy account of how he had ordered a new beer that tasted like lemon cheesecake. The coffee machine buzzed in the background.

'One of my neighbours is making kombucha, I think,' I said.

'That stuff is awful,' said Eddie. 'I had a girlfriend that used to make it in her bedroom.'

I grimaced. 'How did that work out for you?'

'She broke up with me for not having enough hobbies. Apparently caring for my mum made me boring.'

'Ouch,' I said. 'That's not nice. Most people would see it as noble, or, like, a good thing.'

'Hm,' said Eddie. 'What would my therapist say? *People bring their own issues into a situation*, or something like that. But then is that my ex's issue? Am I meant to say *her loss*?'

'The kombucha would have been a dealbreaker for me.'

'It was pretty bad.'

After our smoothies arrived, Eddie said his mother hadn't been well. He was worried he was going to need time off work.

'I'm sure it will be fine,' I said. 'That's what leave is for.'

Eddie smiled and nodded, but I knew I'd been too cold, too quick to deflect his concerns as less than my own. I felt distracted, worried about Chelsea. I peered out the window, scanning the street for a glimpse of her.

I added, 'I'm sorry she's not well, though. That must be really worrying for you.'

That seemed to fix things. Eddie was quite easy to get right, and I didn't like to upset him. When he was disappointed, Eddie pressed his lips together in a straight line until they almost disappeared. He wiped his forehead with a napkin and asked me about work.

The main street was busy for a Sunday afternoon, crammed with people in sunglasses and garish shorts. The windows opposite glinted and reflected the light back so they seemed black, like the rooms behind them had been abandoned. Everyone appeared to be trying to get somewhere, diving between one another, elbowing someone out the way.

A waitress leaned over us to clear the table and placed the bill between us. I had half of my smoothie left, but decided it wasn't worth asking her to leave it. It had tasted thick and muddy.

'What are you doing now?' asked Eddie.

'Shopping,' I lied, to sound like I had something to do. 'What about you?'

He looked sheepish, and worried at one of his fingernails.

'Actually,' he said, 'I was supposed to do these worksheets for my therapist. My appointment is tomorrow.'

'I didn't realise you were seeing someone, like, actively,' I said.

'Just because of my mum, you know. It's good to have some space where I can talk about it.'

'That seems sensible,' I said. 'Although, the homework sounds terrible.'

'You strike me as the kind of person who would *always* do the homework.'

'Oh yeah, but I'd hate every second of it. I just wouldn't want to fail.'

'I don't think you can fail at therapy,' said Eddie.

'Sure you can,' I said. 'That's why people keep on going back.'

Eddie pressed his lips into a thin line.

He insisted on walking with me most of the way up the main street to the supermarket, even though his flat was in the opposite direction. He thought the area was dangerous. He'd told me about someone getting stabbed near my road – a one-off event ten years ago. I told him about places I'd walked to, and he'd say, *You probably shouldn't do that.* Of course, this frightened me, and this was how I'd settled into my route to the park and back, only to be walked in the daylight. But at my most petulant, irritated by Eddie's pandering, I wanted to say that I really wasn't scared of being stabbed, after everything I'd been through. I stopped myself – I knew, from my boyfriend, that I was prone to exaggerating.

When we got to the car park, Eddie waved goodbye. I did a bit of a circle, then made my way back to the flat. I felt exhausted, as I always did when I'd been around people. It was as if I was pretending to be myself, the me I'd been before my boyfriend. I was trying to keep this me – the one who said the wrong thing, the one who could do damage – away from everyone else. If I wasn't careful enough, I'd destroy the little I had left.

That night, I drifted in and out of a feverish sleep. The flat prickled around me, like something terrible had been woken and was searching for me. And then, from the bathroom, a flurry of water spilling from the shower, as though someone had knocked it. I lay still and listened, my heart against my chest. Movement across the floor, from the bathroom into my bedroom – someone tiptoeing around, accidentally falling into the doors, the bed, tripping over the shoes left strewn across the carpet.

I sat up, hoping I was dreaming and could break the spell. The moonlight came through the blinds in sharp lines, glinting blades. A chill ran down my back, as though someone had placed a hand there. It turned me, a slight movement that made me look at the wardrobe.

The door was open, but I was certain I'd left it closed. My clothes rocked on their hangers. I leaped to the door and slammed it shut, throwing my weight against it, almost knocking the wardrobe back. I heard knocking, and felt sure that it was coming from inside, or through the wall.

'Leave me alone,' I whispered.

The knocking stopped.

Later, as I lay on the sofa, watching for the intruder, I thought again about my boyfriend. My mind seemed like a zoetrope of our arguments and how I might have avoided them: the time he tipped over a table and broke things my parents had given me – candle holders, ceramic cats, photo frames; the time I couldn't sleep and rolled over one too many times, so he threw me out of the bedroom and wedged the door shut with our chest of drawers; the hole he punched in the kitchen wall, underneath the window, which I fixed with paper and filler while he slept.

One afternoon, not long after our second anniversary, I was sat on the edge of the bed, and my boyfriend sat opposite me, on the chair in the corner where I folded and left his clothes. The sun came through the window, buttering the side of my face. He sank back into the shadow.

I said, 'We did talk about this.'

He said, 'You're just telling me what you want to happen.'

'We agreed you can go,' I replied, smiling. 'I said you could take the car.'

'*So* kind of you.'

I knew I had made a mistake then. I wanted to be fast enough to stop it. I tried to make myself apologetic; I heard my voice rise into a plea.

'I'm really sorry. It's in the middle of the week – I can't take any more leave.'

'You wouldn't even *have* the car without me.'

I should have left it there. I should have said I was going for a walk, or needed to run an errand – it was such a beautiful day – but I couldn't leave it. I found it so unjust, the way he spoke to me.

'We split things *equally*,' I said, slowly. 'I bought the car before I met you. I insure it.'

He leaned his elbows on his thighs. 'The food?' he said. 'The furniture? All those coffees?'

'I didn't realise we were keeping a ledger.'

'*I'm* not. But you clearly are.'

'Have I ever criticised the way we split things?'

'Nothing is ever good enough for you,' he said. 'You make everything about you.'

'What?' I said.

The room was silent, then. It frightened me how still he could be when he was angry; sometimes I wondered if he was real. I got up and chewed my nails. I tried to keep my voice even.

'Last week, we were eating dinner, and we spoke about this. You mentioned the wedding, and I said I couldn't come. And you said, *Just take some leave.* I explained that I can't, because I'm nearly running out, and I want to save some for the end of the year, for Christmas with your family. And you said, *What will I do, then?* And I said, *Take the car, I'll get the train to work, or a taxi,* and then your phone rang.'

'Do you write this down?' he said.

'I'm just trying to be clear.'

'And trying to make me feel guilty.'

'No.'

'You think you're subtle, but I've never met anyone as *stupid* as you.'

'Don't call me stupid,' I said, quietly.

'Why?'

When I tried to leave the room, he trapped me inside it, holding one hand against the door as I pulled. I finally broke away, tripping down the stairs. He followed, chasing me, I suppose. I ended up on the floor, in a patch of sun like a spotlight. *Dramatic,* he'd said when I'd fallen over. *Do you hate me now,* I'd said, crying, as he pinned me down. I should have learned by then that arguing was pointless; he'd make sure I'd never win.

I hit him back, eventually, very poorly. My hand felt heavy and slow as I brought it to his cheek. I barely touched him, but I wanted to get him off me, because, this time, and every time, I didn't know how it would really end. I knew the patterns of his moods, could tell when I was coaxing him, staving off my next punishment, but I always grew too tired, and slipped. I knew it was inevitable, but I tried my very best, anyway. My lashing out, my audacity, only made it worse, and I knew that it made me as bad as him.

'Why can't you leave it alone?' he sobbed. 'Why have you always got to do this?'

I was not easy to live with. I was unforgiving. After an argument, I didn't want him to touch me. I'd get changed in the bathroom, so he couldn't see my body. I didn't want him to look at me, and he grew angry with me when he saw the bruises he'd made. I reminded him of what he'd done – what I had made him do.

The next day, I'd arrive home from work and fall straight into bed, drained from carrying on, denying what had happened to me. My boyfriend came home later, his commute inexplicably longer, and he would hover at the bedroom door, waiting for me to get up. I did, but I wouldn't kiss him, and if he came back with something to soften the atmosphere – a bouquet of flowers – I'd take them down to the kitchen and leave them on the side, not sure what to do with them. I'd wait for an apology, a real one, and acknowledgement that what had happened was wrong, and wouldn't happen again, but it never came. It would take days for me to feel anything like normal, and then, finally, I'd say, *We just need to learn to communicate more clearly.*

In the morning, I tried to distract myself. I listened for birds, Alice and Sean shouting to each other through their flat as they got ready for work, the dripping tap, but everything was still. I reached outside my thin blanket for my phone, shocked at how much the air felt like a hand around my wrist. I checked my work emails, sipping a strong coffee.

Mark and Liz Walker used the corridor to argue, hissing at one another in lowered voices, thinking Chelsea wouldn't be able to hear them. I provided a false sense of privacy, so quiet they forgot about the thinness of the walls. Once, coming across me in the corridor as I was on my way out for a walk, Liz had jumped and said, *Oh my god. I forgot you were here.*

I heard Mark and Liz leave their flat, and I moved to watch them through the peephole.

'We need to tackle this together,' said Liz.

Mark paused before he answered. 'She does have a point though, doesn't she?' he said. 'She's an adult.'

'She's still living in *our* house, Mark. What if she goes away and speaks to her teachers like that?'

'Lecturers,' said Mark.

'What?' said Liz.

'It's lecturers at university.'

Liz slammed the Walkers' front door. A few minutes later, Mark opened it quietly and padded inside.

I shuddered, unnerved by the unpredictability of the flat, the sound of arguing, so susceptible to noise that I worried myself. I needed, as my boyfriend liked to tell me, to *get a grip*. I opened my laptop, searched the websites for more spells again, looking for an answer. I clicked through so many links I couldn't remember what I was searching for, exactly. As I read, I felt a flicker of dread and looked around the room, certain something had been moving in the corner. But the room was empty, biding its time.

I chastised myself for being so ridiculous. I often felt anxious late at night, afraid of being alone in the dark. If I let this fester and didn't distract myself, I became paranoid that my boyfriend had managed to hack my computer and was watching what I did from afar, laughing at my search history, my hours of scrolling when I couldn't sleep, and ridiculing me with whoever he was fucking now.

Eventually, I found a video. A long-haired blonde woman sat cross-legged on the floor, on a mat, and lit pink-and-white candles, very similar to the ones I'd seen Jess and Chelsea use at the park. The woman's nails were painted like pink-and-white striped sweets. The upper part of her face was deliberately missing from the shot, so you could see her body and her lips, which were bright red.

Her spell sounded like a rhyming poem, and in it she said *banish*, she said *remove*, she said *love*. She explained that the spell was about *removing negative energy, bad influences and aggressive presences*. To me, these all felt like abstract things that she could attribute to the spell by coincidence. Say she felt happy the next day, waking up to the sun; wouldn't that be a coincidence, a natural, human response to stimuli? What if someone she didn't want to speak to finally stopped texting her the day after the spell? What if she just changed her number? To her, would it be proof that the spell had worked?

But the comments below the video piqued my interest. Several users called the spell *wonderful*, and said that it worked. One user commented: *This absolutely banished my shitty ex.* Another wrote: *I swear to god I stopped pining for my terrible ex once I'd cast this spell. Do it!!!* Another comment sounded a little less exact: *This cured my insomnia after two years!* By the end of the video, the woman's eyes were heavy and her speech slow, as though she were falling asleep. In turn, my breath became deeper; I felt light, full of air.

I also realised that I hadn't seen or heard Chelsea crying since Saturday. I'd heard her on the phone, stomping down the stairs, saying, *Yes, I'm fine,* or shouting at Liz, *I'm not upset! Why does everyone act like I'm upset all the time.* Maybe it was true that she was no longer upset. Perhaps the things she and Jess had been doing were intended to heal Chelsea of her heartbreak. What if they'd needed to banish Joseph, a terrible and toxic presence? With some trial and error, they had fixed her. I felt sick at the thought of Joseph and what he might have done to Chelsea. I was sceptical, but knew I had nothing to lose. With all the spells and videos available on the internet, perhaps I might try a similar spell for myself, something to ward off the nightmares, the persistent, intrusive memories of my boyfriend.

Perhaps I could be healed too.

Five

The next day, Tuesday, I worked through a series of complex cases, which I'd been putting off until I had a day without meetings or phone calls. These were tasks that required concentration: hours flipping between multiple tabs, puzzles to be solved. I worked on these in a trance, wearing old shorts and a T-shirt, my bare legs sticking to my computer chair. I surfaced in the late afternoon, stomach growling, feeling parched.

Chelsea's boyfriend, Joseph, returned with sickly pink roses, wrapped in white paper. They looked revolting, like an animal cut open and pulsing.

I heard and saw Joseph before Chelsea did, my windows open to encourage air into the flat. He pulled up in his car, without any music on, prolonging the surprise. Dread swarmed my stomach; I knew how sinister surprises could be.

Joseph stood on the front lawn, looking at the door to the block. The birds chattered, gossiping, and the sky moved as though recorded through a time-lapse. Joseph wore a blue shirt, unbuttoned, which flapped around him. He ran his hand over his hair, which had been shaved since I'd last seen him.

He called Chelsea, looking pleased with himself.

'Will you come down?' he said, almost shouting into the phone.

My stomach fluttered. I heard Chelsea pad down the stairs. There was no urgency in her step, as though she were going down to complete a chore. The windows trembled. She paused at the edge of the lawn, and the birds fell silent.

As I watched from my bedroom window, I waited for something to change – a bang, the floorboards to creak, the smell of earth to seep through the carpet – but the flat was holding its breath.

'Hi,' said Chelsea.

'I got you these,' Joseph said, holding out the bouquet.

Chelsea didn't move. 'That's nice of you.'

She folded her arms over her chest and waited.

Joseph's mouth hung open for a moment before he gently threw the bouquet on the lawn. The flowers flopped sadly.

'I just wanted to see how you're doing,' he said.

'I'm okay,' she replied.

'I was thinking about, well, actually, I don't know. I just wanted to say hi.' He looked at the grass.

'How are you?' Chelsea asked.

'Good. My mum misses you.'

Chelsea laughed, unfolding her arms. 'Does she?'

A gasp escaped me, the reality of the situation becoming clearer. I moved back from the window, hoping they hadn't heard. I could see where this was going. In unfolding her arms, Chelsea was letting him in. I wanted to stop it, to go down there and interrupt, somehow.

'And everyone's been asking about you. They think you've disappeared or something. They want you to come to the party.'

'Oh yeah? I was thinking of going.'

'With me?'

'Maybe.'

'Do you want to go for a drive?' he said, smiling.

Chelsea grinned back. 'Okay.'

She picked up the roses on her way to the car. As they drove off, the birds fled the trees, chasing each other across the clouds.

Down on the street, teenage girls younger than Chelsea were pursued by boys balancing on the rear tyres of their bikes. In the distance, an ice cream van played 'Greensleeves'.

I opened the freezer, looking for ice for my water, and found it had switched off, dripping onto the floor. The clock on the oven flashed as though there had been a power cut, but it wouldn't change when I pressed the buttons to reset it. I flicked the light switches, trying to see if they worked, until one of the bulbs blew. I checked the fuse board in the airing cupboard, but everything looked fine.

Suddenly, I felt that I wasn't alone. The flat grew agitated, rumbling, the floor vibrating, as though it were growling. A snarl moved through the flat, and then a loud bang came from my bedroom.

On my bed, directly below where the light fitting hung: jagged pieces of glass, fallen as though arranged. I moved closer and saw the shards as a set of jaws, a bear trap, ready to snap shut. The light bulb had blown with such force, it had taken the glass of the fitting with it.

The blind shook in the wind and pulsed forward, but whatever had caused the commotion had left. The flat was quiet again, and the heaviness in my body drifted away like a threatening rain cloud. I peered around the door frame into the rest of the flat. The space looked exactly the same as before, but something about its atmosphere had changed, like it too was frightened of what had just happened.

There had been moments, in the first few days after I'd left him, where I'd imagined my boyfriend calling me, asking me to come back. He would have spoken to his GP about his anger; he was going to therapy now. He loved me, and was going to love me like a normal person. This would be the last time, he promised. Instead, he sent me one text before I changed my number: *I can't believe you would do this.* My nightmares and disturbances were so frequent now, growing in violence, I wondered, sometimes, if he'd died and was haunting me, or had discovered where I lived and cursed the flat. I thought of him pressed behind the walls, watching me, creeping inside at night to punish me for escaping. Perhaps I'd never truly be rid of him. He could be vindictive like that.

When I left my boyfriend, I forgot to log out of his computer. As I was trying to sort things out – redirecting bills, changing my address, resetting passwords – I'd discovered that he'd been through my inbox and deleted things. He'd mostly erased messages from years ago – emails from people I no longer kept in touch with, or receipts I was keeping in case. But he'd also flagged and pinned every email I'd ever received from him, so that when I opened my inbox, I'd be confronted by him.

I wanted to understand what had gone wrong, when he had changed, so I read through each one. Our emails were often links to things we found funny, interesting, or wanted to buy, one day, when we could afford it. We had a shared folder for photos of interior design ideas. I signed my emails off with a single kiss; he signed his with his initial. Finally, I had deleted them all. But removing myself from him wasn't such a quick cut; it was like unstitching a seam.

My parents were relieved. They had made every effort with him. My mother baked elaborate cakes for his birthday; my father offered to sort out the garden for us, which was overgrown (my boyfriend said *he* was going to sort it), or fix the car, instead of taking it to a garage, which my boyfriend declined.

'Do they think we're poor?' my boyfriend said.

'We're certainly not wealthy,' I reminded him.

'You don't think I do enough, do you? You'd be happier with someone rich.'

'Of course not. They're just trying to help us. They're being kind.'

My boyfriend hated my parents. He refused their invitations to stay with them for the weekend, so I'd have to go alone, making excuses for him. He'd be cold with me when I returned, annoyed that I had chosen to spend time with them instead of him. Eventually, I capitulated, and stopped visiting. I found it easier not to talk about them around him. I called my parents infrequently and in secret, pretending I was fine and busy, hanging up as soon as I heard his keys being slotted into the door. Because we knew the passwords to each other's phones, it wasn't safe to text my parents, or anyone, about him. Good or bad, he wouldn't have liked it.

There were, of course, wonderful things. There had to be. He could be so affectionate, it shocked me. If I fell asleep on him, with my mouth open, and left a wet patch on his T-shirt, he would laugh and say, *I love you*, so tenderly, like I was incapable of doing wrong. The night before my birthday, he stayed up late to decorate the house with flowers, paper garlands, and created playlists of my favourite songs for me to open my presents to. On days when I felt too tired, or sore, he brushed my hair for me.

I felt as though I had lived with two people: the boyfriend before we lived together, and the one who appeared the moment the last box came inside, when the front door was closed.

Not long after we started dating, I had a terrible sickness bug and told him to stay away. It was early in February. The wind howled and the rain came down in sheets, like it was slapping the tarmac. The windows tremored in their frames. I shivered in my bed, listening to my housemate argue with his girlfriend about her flirting with someone at a party. I must have drifted to sleep and was woken by my boyfriend gently tapping on my bedroom door. When I opened it, he covered his face with a plastic bag of crackers, plain crisps and white rice that he was going to cook for me until I felt better.

At that point, I wasn't certain what we were doing; we had been having sex, frequently, but we hadn't spoken about a relationship. I assumed he wouldn't want one.

'Don't come near me,' I told him. 'I'm gross.'

I was ashamed because I was probably still contagious and hadn't bathed in days.

'Don't be silly,' he'd said, kissing my forehead.

Then he'd taken me to the bathroom and lowered me into the bath, and washed me with lukewarm water and a sponge. As I lay there with my eyes closed, I realised I trusted him, and probably loved him. I'd thought that people who were just fucking didn't do this kind of thing for each other, and he must have really liked me, too, then.

It was hard to reconcile those people with the ones we became when we moved in together. Sometimes I'd walk into the room and he'd just be sitting there, in the darkness, waiting for me.

I understood what it was to be helplessly in love. When we first began dating, I tried things he liked because he liked them — certain music, a pub he loved but I found grimy, television programmes I swore I'd never watch. I wanted to share those things with him, and I wanted to be loved, and liking the things he liked always made him like me more: more laughter, more time with me, more rewards for my good behaviour. These minor changes in taste didn't feel threatening at the time. In love, I exposed myself to all kinds of attacks. This, of course, was an extreme. Not all love is a direct attack; it might be a slow infiltration.

I was scared that we would run out of new things to tell each other, that he'd eventually find me boring. As we approached our third anniversary, I was filled with horror when I discovered something new about him from someone else. I was most disturbed when the new information somehow contradicted the version of him I knew. At the pub one night, a mutual friend mentioned the girlfriend he'd had a year before me. I'd been told nothing about this person, in fact he'd said that before meeting me he had been 'happily single' for two years.

'Who was she?' I asked him on the train home, swaying against the turbulence, my hand slipping on the handrail.

He looked at our reflections flickering in the train windows and said, 'Not a real girlfriend.'

He continued to stare at me in the mirror of the window until I looked away.

I allowed myself to be placated. I supposed he had been honest. If he really didn't regard her as a girlfriend, then he hadn't lied.

Every time I discovered an untruth, I accepted that he hadn't deceived me, not really, or ruminated until I could understand why he'd been dishonest – I was, after all, difficult about these things. *You're being sensitive*, he said. *I knew you'd get upset.*

In living like this, I permitted boundaries to be blurred, the outside to come in, until I couldn't remember what was real and what he'd made up. At the end of it all, I couldn't be sure I was seeing things as they were.

Chelsea returned much later, darkness and the residual heat of the day smothering the building. Outside, the wind disturbed the trees, beckoning a storm. As Chelsea stepped onto the front lawn, the lights flickered back on and the kettle crackled, as though the flat had been waiting for her.

Chelsea was escorted by a police officer, clutching to her chest the roses Joseph had given her. Through the peephole,

I watched them come down the corridor to the Walkers' flat, the police officer's boots thudding against the carpet. There was a pit in my stomach; I swallowed bile. My heart beat so furiously, I felt it might knock me over.

Chelsea tapped on the Walkers' door, as though the sound would be more offensive than the scene. Odd that she didn't let herself in. Her hair hung over her face, so I couldn't read her expression. The police officer stepped back, mute. Chelsea looked over her shoulder.

Liz unlocked the door and took in Chelsea, then the officer.

'Hello?' Liz said, as though Chelsea was a stranger.

'Mum,' said Chelsea, voice hoarse and thick from crying.

'Where have you been?' Liz said this quietly, as if she didn't want to be overheard.

I kept still, hoping they hadn't heard me move behind the door. A garbled sound left Chelsea's mouth.

'Can we have a chat?' the police officer interjected.

Liz looked up at the man, her nose wrinkled with confusion, terror. She cleared her throat. Chelsea looked at her shoes. The roses were crushed on one side, as if they'd been used as a weapon.

'Just a quick chat with you and Chelsea,' the police officer said.

Liz considered this.

'Your dad's in,' she said. A message for the officer, a warning.

The officer nodded.

Chelsea looked back at him again before stepping towards Liz. I saw a patch of her cheek, blotchy and uneven, angry.

Before she was inside, I was certain that she peeked up and glanced at my door, as though she could feel me there.

Their voices faded as they walked into the flat and shut the door. I waited by the peephole for a while, hoping to hear something. Not long after, Alice and Sean returned home, laughing and drunk. They started playing video games, gunshots pulsing through the building.

The policeman remained inside the Walkers' flat. It was obvious what had happened. Chelsea and her boyfriend had gone out for the day. At some point, she'd made a mistake, like bringing up something he'd done in the past, accidentally goading him, or maybe deliberately, wanting to make a point about the way he treated her — as though he could discard her and pick her up when he wanted. She didn't like that. Perhaps she'd seen something on his phone. This seemed probable; they were always on their phones. During their argument, Joseph had become irate. Chelsea had said something she'd regret later on — something cutting, something only she knew could wound him. And then he'd shoved her, maybe, or worse. Perhaps he had abandoned her wherever they'd gone, and she'd had to find her way home — this would explain why the police had escorted her. She wouldn't have wanted to tell them what had happened, but there could be no avoiding it now. Joseph was hurting her.

Several minutes later, the police officer pulled the Walkers' door shut. He whistled as he walked away, down the stairs. At the same time, the flat roared: a noise, like someone pushing over furniture, crashed through the ceiling, as though the world were being torn. Then the thud of footsteps, like someone was racing down a set of stairs towards me. I froze, expecting something to appear, to happen. A grating sound came from my walls, as though someone was trying to get to me.

I ran to my bed and hid under the sheet, my pulse throbbing in my temples. I couldn't bear much more of this torment: the noises, the sense that the flat wasn't safe, that my boyfriend was going to find me, and then what? It had been ten months since I had left him, and I had to do something about it. Whatever I did had to be definitive, resolute, so that he couldn't come back. Whatever Chelsea and Jess had conducted the other night had not worked; this was obvious. I needed something more potent, more deliberate – something that would expel my boyfriend for ever. And then, maybe Chelsea's boyfriend, too.

After a few hours of clicking around, I found something called a cord-cutting spell, which was intended for the worst of break-ups; it could stop thoughts about a person for good. It sounded complicated, but achievable. There were many things I needed, and I knew very little about them. A black candle, white sage, Florida Water, several metres of black cotton thread, scissors. What I had: a half-burned white candle with a skeleton poking out, sage leaves, tap water, a half-empty reel of black cotton. Scissors didn't feel involved enough for what I wanted to do, so I found a paring knife. I googled Florida Water and concluded that it was like perfume. I searched through my drawers until I found a tiny glass bottle, with a drop of *eau de parfum* left inside. I sprayed it around the rooms, expelling my boyfriend.

I opened the windows. Gusts of wind unsettled the blinds, and the walls creaked in response. Heavy clouds choked the sky. I removed the batteries from the fire alarms, and then, in a dish, I set fire to the sage leaves, which stayed whole and charred. I crumbled the leaves in my fingers until my hands were coated in charcoal.

I completed the routine in my bathroom. I didn't trust myself not to accidentally set myself on fire – I wanted to be close to water. I sat in the bath, cross-legged, my knees up against the sides, and placed the candle in between my legs. I focused, at first, on the sounds of my neighbours moving around beneath me: dragging their chairs across the floor, slamming cupboard doors, the muffled applause coming from their televisions. Thunder rolled overhead. And then I let each sound fall away, as though it wasn't really there. The flat heard my wishes and listened, droning quietly in the background.

I lit the candle, and then I closed my eyes and thought about my boyfriend, of cutting his hair in our bathroom. I had done this many times for friends, but it took a while to convince him to allow me to do it. It only happened once. After I'd finished, he'd stood in front of the mirror, studying his reflection. He got close to the glass, his nose almost against it. *Do you think this looks stupid?* he said. *This bit seems longer than the rest.* I knew it couldn't be because I had checked it thoroughly. He stayed there a while, preening. One of his hairs had got stuck between my teeth. I ran my tongue over it all evening, trying to get it out.

I found the reel of cotton and unwound it, and halved it. Then I knotted it, several times, and made it look something like a rosary: a knot for each thing I wanted to forget about him. The scent of the candle – like moss and damp earth – filled the room. Rain tapped at the windows. I wound the first half of the cotton length tightly around my ankles, until it felt like it was cutting into my skin. I chanted the words of the spell. I felt ridiculous, and the flat hummed a little more loudly in agreement, then hushed itself. I felt my breath tighten, a hand wound itself around my neck, then loosened its grip.

I had to bind my wrists together too. I lay the cotton over them and wrapped my tongue under the thread to pull it into a loop. I tightened it and tied the final knot with my teeth, making sure the bind was close to my skin. I counted the knots and recited each moment I wanted to forget. My voice was thin, and I cleared my throat to try again, but it came out hoarse.

When I was done, I slipped the knife into the knots around my wrists, splitting as many as possible before the cotton frayed and fell. I could be more careful with the bind around my ankles and took time to prise the knots apart carefully, like I was slicing blood vessels and gristle from meat. Then I sprayed myself with the perfume, filling the room with lavender and almond. I was too generous, my hands shaking, and inhaled some of it. I spluttered until my eyes watered and turned to real tears. My sobs echoed around the bathroom. The rain responded by crashing against the window. I wondered if I had done something wrong, if I had missed something important. I did all this quickly, glancing up at the bathroom door, half-expecting my boyfriend to walk in and catch me at any moment.

I held the threads over the candle. My fingernails were blue with cold, despite the humidity of the storm. I was meant to collect the ashes of the thread, but I couldn't salvage much. I wrapped the small amount I had in tissue and used a bit of remaining thread to tie it up. I wrapped myself in a raincoat and left the flat to finish the ritual.

As I entered the park, the wind pushed me backwards. The trees tilted like they were throwing their heads back, screaming, their hair flying wildly behind them. I climbed up the hill, using my hands to steady me. Mud and water swelled up wherever I touched. Wind like someone running down the stairs. Wind like a body thrown against a door.

Under the trees, the air slowed and became icy, a glass pressed against skin. I used my hands to dig a hole, dirt clinging to my nails. I made sure it was deep. Out of respect, out of fear of disturbing something I might not understand, I made sure I wasn't too close to Chelsea's stone. I untied the tissue but left the ashes inside, and pressed it as far down as it would go. I kicked earth over the top of the hole once it was filled and smelt the perfume rising from the ground.

I turned and watched the lights in the houses flicker on. Someone came out their front door and checked that their car was locked; the lights blinked as the alarm turned off and back on. Above, the clouds parted, and the moon was a sliver of white-hot flame in the sky. The wind put a hand to my back and guided me home.

Six

The next evening, Eddie texted: *Are you okay? Do you need anything?* I had called in sick to work that morning, ravaged by a fever. The news must have spread to Eddie. I meant to reply, but I slipped between dream and being awake without being able to tell the two apart. I felt my boyfriend hovering over me, or heard him crashing through the door. I was trapped in the house we'd shared, and when I opened my eyes, I tried to remind myself I was safe before sleep smothered me again. I woke up with scratches over my chest and arms. I had bled onto the sheets. When I tried to move around the flat, my legs buckled, and I crawled instead. In the moments I was awake, and lucid, I typed out responses asking Eddie for help – some plain food for when I was feeling better, or, actually, could he just come over and make sure I didn't die – but deleted them.

Lying there, I was certain that I had done the spell wrong and that my boyfriend was now coming for me, that I had called him to me, instead of exorcising him. I tortured myself by ruminating on direct examples of my boyfriend's erratic and unpredictable behaviour, case studies I placed alongside one another. I thought of the incident where I'd had flu, falling in love while my boyfriend bathed me, my mind presented another occasion as fact. Not long after I'd moved into his house, I had been unwell again. I was always coming down with things back then: persistent infections that couldn't be remedied, colds, and a near-constant feeling of nausea. When I visited my doctor, she said, *Are you stressed?* I supposed I was. I attributed the illnesses to work.

We were supposed to meet friends for dinner. We had been seeing less of them. I thought this was because we were settling down, having been together for three years at that point. Some of them had babies, were getting married. We couldn't go to the pub like that anymore. We had spoken about marriage, but it was something that was definitely going to happen later. That night, my boyfriend went out drinking without me, and I took a shallow lukewarm bath, trying to ward off the fever. Then I sat on the bathroom floor in my towel, crying like an injured dog, my skin hot to the touch. It hurt to wear anything, and when I lay on my side, I felt as though my knees were grinding against each other. I eventually crawled back to bed, and waited for him to return.

I knew he wasn't pleased. There was always tension when we were due to do something social. I became eager to please, too clingy. He became distant, cold. When we were out together, it would feel as though he was repulsed by me; I'd panic when I couldn't get him to catch my eye, or when he wouldn't put his arm around me, or when he turned away from me, leaving me out of the conversation. And here I was, ruining another night.

I shouldn't have been surprised when he came back, the acrid smell of vomit clinging to his coat, and spat at me, in the dark, 'You couldn't even make an effort. You never try. This is why everyone is sick of you.'

His sudden hatred was always devastating, like something precious had been destroyed beyond repair. He hung over me, goading me. There was no option to stay quiet, or pretend I was asleep, and whatever I eventually said – an apology, a plea – would make it worse. Then, the mattress was ripped from under me, completely off the bed, and I was swaying by the window, on the wrong side of the room, as he stood between me and the door.

I finally texted Eddie for help that evening, when the nightmares wouldn't break. The sky leaked red, a cut being washed. He arrived what felt like hours later, but it was still light outside. The little grey screen in my intercom was blurry and dark, and as I picked up the phone and the image bloomed, Eddie appeared indistinctly, like an apparition captured on an old camera. I buzzed him in and waited for him by my door. When he didn't turn up, I called his phone, but it went straight to voicemail. I slid down to the floor and waited for him there, feeling the thrum of my pulse in my head, and the flat groaning in time.

'I got a bit lost,' he said through the door. 'Your neighbour let me in.'

'The intercom,' I said, rocking.

'I met her outside,' he said. 'The girl?'

I reached up to unlock the door, and Eddie pushed it open.

Once I was back in bed, Eddie wandered around the flat, making me glasses of iced water, giving me painkillers, bringing me damp towels for my forehead. I wanted to sleep again, but he tried to put things away in my cupboards, opening and closing the doors several times. A hollow echo rang out every time the door banged shut. Eddie's feet felt heavy against the floor and shook the frames on the walls. My legs ached, and I felt as though someone were pressing the sides of my head.

Eddie left a packet of Rich Tea biscuits next to the bed and then sat in the living room for a few hours, with the television lowly murmuring in the background.

'I just want to be sure you're not going to get worse,' he said, at some point, from the bedroom door.

'I'm sorry,' I said. 'What about your mum?'

'The community carers are coming out this evening. I'll check on her on my way home.'

Later, when I felt stronger, I joined him in the living room. He muted the regional news and moved over on the sofa, so I could sit down.

'Thank you,' I said.

'It's fine,' he said. 'You don't have anything to watch.'

'I keep on meaning to set up a subscription.'

Eddie looked around. 'There's a strange smell in here. Do you want me to find it before I go?'

'What smell?' I asked. I wondered if it was me.

'Just damp. Probably something wrong with the extractor.'

'It's all right. You can go.'

'Just a bit longer,' he said, unmuting the television.

We listened to the final story. A man had murdered his wife and left the weapons – several knives, a cleaver – in his car. His neighbours had reported him to the police, seeing the weapons on the back seat, covered in blood.

'Can we turn this off?' I said.

'Sure,' said Eddie, waiting until the story was finished.

I slept deeply, without dreaming, and woke up to a hand flashing across my back. I blinked in the darkness, holding my breath, waiting for my boyfriend's figure to lean over me, or for the room to change. Someone's breath whistled at the back of my neck.

'What did you do?' the voice hissed.

I rolled over and met a face that, in shadow, looked like my own.

I blinked, and Chelsea came into focus. She kneeled on the mattress. The room was swimming as though shrouded in heat, and smelt of fresh earth. The flat clicked like an old gas hob, impatient at having been woken up.

'What?' I said.

'Your *friend* said you were unwell.' She handed me a glass of water from down the side of the bed.

'Did he let you in?'

'No,' she said. 'I let myself in.'

I didn't want to sound alarmed. 'I didn't know you could do that.'

'Oh my god, no,' Chelsea snorted. 'We have an old spare key. My mum and dad were friends with the people who lived here before. They took in their parcels sometimes.'

'I should probably talk to the landlord about that,' I said.

I wondered if I was dreaming. Chelsea and I had never spoken before, not even to greet each other in the corridor, and now she was in my flat.

'So what did you do?' she said. 'I know you've been watching us.'

I sat up and sipped the water, giving myself some time before answering. Chelsea didn't look well herself – her forehead was beaded with sweat, and she was pale. She rolled up the sleeves of her hoodie.

'Cord-cutting,' I said, finally.

'Fucking hell.'

'I think I must have done something wrong.'

'Show me what you did,' she said.

I led her into the bathroom and showed her the remnants of my spell. As she picked up the perfume bottle, she laughed and said, 'Oh god,' under her breath. I leaned against the door frame, steadying my breathing. The tiles were cold against my feet. It felt strange yet inevitable that she was here, and that we were talking about spells. I wondered what she'd said to Eddie, and how she'd justified letting herself in. I didn't know whether to be alarmed or grateful.

I looked at Chelsea and myself in the mirror. Pale. Cracked, reddening lips. Flushed cheeks. We looked, in the darkness, quite similar.

'Where did you bury it?' Chelsea said. She breathed out with pursed lips, as though smoking, and settled on the edge of the bath.

'The park,' I said.

Chelsea looked at me and sighed. 'Fine.'

It occurred to me that she was exaggerating. She was enjoying telling me off. I was, after all, older than her. Whatever her perception of me, she must have known, looking at my condition, that I was going to take her advice seriously. She must have felt, with some glimmer of pride, that I – a woman of twenty-six – respected her.

She got up and moved back into the bedroom, and I followed closely. Her hair was damp at her neck. She sat on my bed, and I understood that I was to sit down too. The moonlight caught her outline and made her appear smaller, then, and less frightening. The flat droned, and the pipes clanged, as if it wanted to have its say on the matter.

'Don't use the wrong things,' Chelsea said. 'It just makes it worse. That smell? That's a sign it's gone wrong.'

'I feel awful,' I said, pressing my hands to my eyes. I massaged them, hoping that I was still dreaming, and that I'd wake up soon, feeling well again.

'I mean, cord-cutting is for when you're *really* unhappy,' she said.

I felt my face burning and drained the water.

Chelsea must have realised I was not going to respond to her probing.

'Have you done this before?' she said, after a pause.

'Not really.'

'Yeah, you have a *fresh* energy about you.'

I had no idea what that meant.

'We're going to have to fix this,' she said.

I realised she was dialling up the gravity in her voice. I tried not to laugh. I didn't really understand what I'd done, but felt that this situation was absurd. I'd burned some objects and now felt like I was dying. I hadn't even decided if I really thought magic was possible.

'Okay,' I said. I suddenly felt exhausted, and wanted to lie back down.

'We'll sort it out tomorrow. Will you be okay for the rest of the night?'

'I think so.'

'Don't worry. The first time I tried to *bond* with a boy I liked, I ended up with food poisoning for a week.'

'Are *you* okay?' I asked.

She blinked at me, either unsure or deliberately evasive.

'The police officer the other day?'

Chelsea waved her hand as though swatting a wasp. She avoided my gaze. 'That was just a misunderstanding.'

'It looked quite serious,' I said.

Chelsea frowned. I knew not to push her further.

'Well, I'm glad everything's okay,' I smiled weakly.

Before I could say anything else, she'd slipped from the bedroom and was out the front door, locking it behind her.

By morning, my fever was subsiding, but still trembling across my head and chest. I couldn't sleep and was uncertain of how much time had passed. I wasn't entirely sure that I hadn't dreamed that Chelsea had let herself into my flat.

The sun streamed through the windows, bright and cleansing. I sat on my sofa with a blanket, listening to the birds singing loudly and happily, and the traffic racing down the road. It felt like everyone was outside, living, and I wanted to join them.

Then, dusk fell, and the sky deepened to violet and yellow, like a bruise. I was so exhausted, I felt like I was hallucinating, not really inside my body.

Someone tapped on my front door – a sort of code, as if they were only using their fingernails.

Chelsea slipped inside when I opened the door, and handed me the spare key. 'I wouldn't have done that usually,' she said. 'But it was an emergency. Sorry.'

'Thanks.'

'Are you ready?' she said, looking me up and down.

I was wearing my pyjamas still; my hair was piled on top of my head and unwashed.

Chelsea didn't look well. She'd tried to cover her face in a slightly darker powder to mask her pallor, but her lips were cracked, and she continued sweating.

'Fine, you'll do it here,' she said.

'Okay,' I said. I blinked at her, hoping she'd explain.

She walked through to the living room and threw herself down on the sofa, sending sprinkles of faux leather into the air. I sat on the floor. Out of her tote bag, Chelsea pulled a plastic clock. It was yellow and red, clearly a children's toy: it had an open face, so the hands could be moved. She also brought out a reel of black cotton and a lighter.

'Very basic,' she said. 'But you're going to reset it. It's easy.'

I nodded, and opened my mouth to ask a question, but Chelsea was ahead of me.

'As late as possible,' she continued. 'Maybe like two or three. Go somewhere quiet – the bathroom will be fine – and sit with the clock. Think about undoing the spell. You can, I don't know, visualise it being undone, or whatever works for you. My friend likes to imagine it as a film, so you can rewind or fast-forward it.'

'Is that your friend who comes here?' I asked. 'Dark hair?'

Chelsea held my eye for a few moments.

'Yes,' she said. 'When you're ready, you unwind the thread a few feet. Keep thinking about undoing the cord-cutting. Then move the clock back fifteen minutes. Unwind, move back fifteen minutes. Do that until you've set the clock back an hour, and then burn the thread.'

I nodded and repeated the instructions back to her.

'Where do I bury it?' I said.

'What?'

'The thread?'

Chelsea laughed. 'You don't need to bury anything this time. Stay inside. Just leave the clock alone once you're done and I'll come back for it.'

'I could leave it outside the door?'

Chelsea shook her head and rolled her eyes. 'No, someone will see it.'

She was incredibly relaxed, and I wondered if it was – like last night – a bit of an act to put me at ease.

She said, 'You'll be fine, honestly. Just don't fuck this one up.'

'Are you sure you're okay?' I said, noticing she was breathing more heavily.

She sniffed and tucked her hair behind her ears. 'Just hay fever,' she said.

The flat clicked and became warmer, like someone was gently heating milk. It was dark outside now, and the moon cast a square of ghostly light onto the carpet.

'How long have you been doing this?' I asked.

'A while,' she said. 'Jess, my friend, introduced me to it.'

'It's much more complicated than I thought.'

'You shouldn't be trying this unless you really know what you're doing.'

'Sorry. I feel ridiculous.'

'You say sorry a lot,' Chelsea said.

'Because I am,' I said.

'Well, as my mum likes to say to my dad, the best apology is a change in behaviour.'

'She's probably right.'

There was a rule I knew but hadn't mastered when I was with my boyfriend: when said repeatedly throughout the day, or over many days, *sorry* became irritating. It was annoying to me – I had felt frustrated at not being able to get it right, and annoyed with myself for fawning over him. My boyfriend was also angry with me, for failing again. But it was especially frustrating to me if my boyfriend did not apologise for his own behaviour. I rarely felt that I was entirely in the wrong, and he knew that by saying sorry, I was hoping to prise an apology from him, from his mouth. My boyfriend didn't know what to do with *sorry*, with remorse, and turned it back on me, punishing me for it.

Chelsea's phone started ringing. She didn't move. I pretended I needed something and went into the bedroom to give her some privacy. I felt that there was something she wanted to say to me but hadn't quite figured out how to broach it, yet.

I had avoided allowing anyone into the flat for a long time, and now, in the same day, I'd had two visitors. The flat had been quieter than usual today – clicks instead of bangs, fewer scrapes against the walls. The fridge was moaning, rather than screeching. It felt strange to have let someone in, to have said: this is how I live.

I looked around my bedroom and saw it through Chelsea's eyes: the empty shelves, the fraying carpet, the dusty curtains. Sad and gloomy. In need of more personal objects. I would get a plant when I felt better.

I could hear Chelsea speaking – 'Now? Okay.'

'My boyfriend's here,' she called.

She picked up her tote bag and stood.

'I thought . . . didn't you break up?' I said.

'God, nothing's private here.'

'Sorry.'

'It was just an argument – happens all the time. You must know that, living here.'

I looked at her quizzically.

'Come on, my mum and dad argue *constantly*. But obviously everything's going to be fine – with them and us. We're just figuring things out.'

She made her way to the front door. I followed, tempted to grab her arm to make her stay. She turned to me one final time before leaving.

'You'll be okay,' she said, smiling, which made me think she meant it.

Finding Joseph's Instagram profile took some work. Chelsea had deleted every trace of him from her account when they'd broken up, and so many people left fire or heart emojis under Chelsea's photos that I had to click on each one, trying to remember usernames. I also got distracted, tempted to look up my boyfriend's name, my old friends. I wondered if

I'd find anything of myself still there – old photographs, a comment from a few years ago. But I felt even more afraid now of the spell. I couldn't trust that searching a name on a website wouldn't somehow bring my boyfriend back into my life. Whatever was happening to me, I believed my anonymity was protection, and couldn't bear to make myself vulnerable again.

The majority of Joseph's photos had been filtered to look as though they were taken on a disposable camera. In his latest post, he was drinking, in a dark kitchen, with friends. White light reflected from the fridge and caught a girl swigging from a bottle of rosé. She was wearing white, and the grainy quality of the photo made her appear to be drawn in chalk, hanging in the corner spectrally. On the other side of the photo, Joseph emerged from the dark corner, sitting backwards on a fold-out chair. He was wearing an Adidas tracksuit, pointing finger guns at the camera, and surrounded by half-drunk bottles containing bright red and green liquid.

Joseph was often with girls in his photos – none of them Chelsea. While I knew that boys could be friends with girls, there was something in the way that the girls leaned on him, commented things like *cute* and used purple heart emojis, that created a sense of everyone being in love with him.

I scrolled down and found a picture of him and Liz, Chelsea's mum. Perhaps he had forgotten to delete it when he and Chelsea had first broken up. Perhaps he didn't do that; maybe he knew they'd get back together. In the photo, Liz and Joseph were in front of a plain white wall, both holding glasses of Aperol spritz. He'd captioned it: *the best drinking partner.* Liz's lipstick was slightly smudged; Joseph's face was flushed. I wondered if Chelsea had taken the photo. Later, cut with moonlight, Chelsea stalked across the front lawn to the door. There was a horrible thud in the bedroom, as though something had dropped down dead, but there was nothing to see, nothing even under the bed. A sense of alarm ran through my body, like I'd been sliced from shoulder to hip, and I made my way to the bedroom window, nostrils flaring, smelling burning meat.

'Every time!' Chelsea said. 'You just can't leave it.'

'What is wrong with you,' Joseph spat.

He was standing on the edge of the lawn, as though there were a barrier to prevent him taking a step forward. Chelsea stood in the middle of the grass. The wind picked up, throwing her hair behind her. My ears rang and pulsed, like something had disturbed them.

'You *never* apologise,' said Chelsea.

'I'm not doing this with you,' he said.

'Okay, yeah, I'm being unreasonable now.'

'I can't talk to you when you're like this.'

Chelsea threw her handbag – small, and black snakeskin – at Joseph. He didn't flinch.

'Where is this coming from?' Chelsea said, crying.

She wrapped her arms around herself and looked, for the first time, very young. Their argument sounded like the argument of every couple, at some point, when the façade crumbles and the childishness seeps out. There had been times when I argued with my boyfriend like this, and I would have been ashamed for someone to witness it – which they did, at parties, or when we were out shopping.

All my pleading and managing of him exacerbated things – I knew I would suffer later. When I thought about these incidents, I pictured myself as small and pale, clinging to his arm, eyes watering. Chelsea hadn't yet learned that crying made everything worse.

'Just go inside,' Joseph said.

'No, I want to talk,' Chelsea said.

'Not when you're like this.'

'But I'm not doing anything.'

'Look at you,' Joseph said.

'Sorry,' said Chelsea. 'I'm really sorry, I don't want to argue.'

Joseph sighed and rolled his eyes. 'Neither do I, Chels, but you can't help it. You've always got to start it.'

These exchanges felt rehearsed, as though they were replaying a scene from a drama, with dialogue that wasn't real. It was an act that had happened many times – they knew the rhythms of this argument, and returned to it, futilely lashing out. I felt exhausted by it already and wondered how Chelsea could cope.

The slam of Joseph's car door echoed around my bedroom. A slammed door could signal finality, but mostly it suggested terrible things to come. Something would have to be done about Joseph.

Chelsea sobbed as she came up the stairs, the sound catching in her throat, like she was inhaling smoke. The burning smell was rotting, creeping through the building. I watched her through the peephole, kicking her shoes off slowly, leaning against the wall and taking deep breaths to calm herself.

She frightened me then, because I knew that sort of crying. There had been times I had spoken out loud to myself while weeping, kneeling at the top of the stairs, a sort of *nonononononononono* when I knew things were bad and I wasn't sure how I was going to fix them. When I cried like that, I thought I didn't sound like myself: this wasn't me; I didn't do this; I didn't plead with anyone. I'd listen to myself, feeling ashamed and horrified. I'd resolve not to be like it again, and then we'd be on the motorway, on our way to something nice, and he'd say, after some little disagreement, *I think there is something seriously wrong with you*, and as I said, *What?* starting the argument for real, I'd think, *Maybe there is.*

I collected the toy clock, and the thread, and sat on the edge of my bed, biding my time until I could rid myself of him.

Seven

I finally felt better the next day, and returned to my spread-sheets. People from down the road had stopped in front of the block to talk about their gardens as July drew to a close. A toddler rode around on his tricycle, scraping the pavement. The sky was ocean-blue, breaths of cloud floating by. I'd woken, for the first time in a long time, with a sense of purpose, having finally spoken to Chelsea. I was eager to learn as much as I could, to figure out how I might banish my boyfriend from my life.

I called my mother, telling her I had been unwell but was mostly recovered now.

'You didn't have to move so far away,' she said, as usual. 'If you were closer, we could help you. You need your independence, I understand, darling. But I really don't think he'll do anything to you, not now. It would be safe to come back.'

When she spoke like this, gestured towards my boyfriend, I felt convulsions of anger, like a door had slammed somewhere inside me. How would anyone else know what my boyfriend would or wouldn't do? I alone had dealt with him, and had seen how he could behave.

She continued: 'He's probably ashamed, as he should be. He must know that you'll have told people what he's like.'

I ended the call shortly after this, once my mother had described the weather for me. She was disappointed that smudges of clouds had been thumbed across the sky, despite the sweltering temperatures, and proclaimed to be sick of the sound of the ice cream van. *It actually turns my stomach!* she declared.

I was lying stretched out on the sofa, windows thrown open, trying to cool down. I'd used all the ice I'd made in tall glasses of water, then crunched the remainder of the cubes. I was listening for Chelsea, hoping to catch her. All day, the Walkers' front door hadn't opened, and that flat had lay dormant. I'd heard Liz and Mark through the walls, at first fiddling with their guitars tunelessly, sounding like they were playing experimental jazz. Then they had abruptly stopped, and talked in low, murmuring voices. Their words were indistinct, but their tones suggested concern, a fraught conversation, rising and falling every so often, like waves. And when that conversation had ended, Liz had clearly called Chelsea to join them.

Chelsea cried, a sort of wail, as Mark and Liz spoke to her. I heard Liz's voice the most, coaxing, reassuring. Mark joined in with monosyllables. I hoped they were talking about Joseph, having an honest conversation about his behaviour, the incident with the police. Surely, they must be, in some way, forbidding her from seeing him? But I knew, from having that conversation with my parents, several times, that one wrong word could derail it all. *It might get better*, I thought, and Chelsea thought; *What if I could change things to make it better?*

Then, the click of the Walkers' door. Mark and Liz were in the corridor again, hissing at one another.

'This is what I mean, Mark,' Liz said. 'You *never* back me up.'

'I did!'

'She was *looking* at you, waiting for you to say something. Children need to feel that their parents are a team.'

'Ah, but we're not, are we?' said Mark. 'That's the whole point.'

There was a moment of silence, then Liz began again. 'Don't you dare blame me for this. I know you won't do it for me, but you can at least do it for your daughter. She's suffering.'

Another slammed door, a short moment, and then some steps inside. Silence fell in the Walkers' flat. As I waited for the conversation to resume, or for the TV to be turned on to signal the end of it, the intercom rang. I jumped and steadied myself before making my way to the screen. There were two shadowy figures in the small box, a man and a woman. The woman tucked her hair behind her ear, and then I recognised her as Alice. She was talking animatedly to the man, who I could tell was not Sean, even though he had his head to the back of the screen.

'Hello,' I said into the phone.

'Oh, hi!' said Alice, so loudly I had to move the phone away from my ear.

Eddie turned to face the camera and waved at me.

'I was trying to let your friend in,' said Alice. 'But I think he's already called the flat, so you need to buzz us in, you know?'

'No,' I said, as the image cut out. I pressed the button to let them inside but was too late. Eddie rang the intercom again. 'Sorry,' I said, pressing the button quickly this time.

'Thank you!' called Alice over her shoulder. Before I hung up, I saw she was carrying a Monstera plant. The leaves writhed in her arms. Eddie followed her closely, reaching over her head to push the door open.

I was bewildered, and the flat seemed to be too: the microwave flickered on and off, beeping every time the power resumed. I pulled the plug from the socket. I'd need to check the fuse later, I thought, trying to ignore the feeling that someone was lurking, ready to pounce. I thought that, because of my illness, Eddie believed that our friendship had now moved into another realm, one in which he would just pop by, unannounced, to see if I was available. And maybe he was right. I'd never had friends that did that, not even when I was at school; things had always been arranged, even if an hour or so beforehand.

I wasn't prepared for a visitor and was wearing an outfit I reserved for the hottest days, and would rather not have been seen in: a pair of cream linen shorts and a white cami-sole. Still, I told myself, I was not sure a friend had ever cared for me when I was unwell, and I was, I supposed, grateful to Eddie.

When I'd been with my boyfriend, I'd neglected my friendships. I was too eager to let him be everything in my life to begin with, and then it took all my energy to manage him, so I couldn't face them. He hid the bruises on the parts of my body that my clothes would cover, so that wasn't a problem; the stray thumbprint-sized ones on my arms attributed to my clumsiness if anyone asked, which no one did.

After arguments, I promised myself space from him – I made lists of people to contact, so that I would have plans when he was going out; I told myself I would join pottery and dance classes I'd researched. Then another evening alone. Flicking through channels, watching a terrible film. Forgetting to make myself dinner. Waiting for my boyfriend to come home, deciding whether to pretend to be asleep or not. I'd realise weeks had passed and I still hadn't made a firm arrangement with anyone.

There had been a period when I tried to make my boyfriend socialise with my friends, as I would with his. One evening, we met mine in the pub – someone's birthday, a low-key affair. I worked late and emerged from the cool of the office's air conditioning into the lingering heat of the day. My skin felt sticky before long. I'd arranged to meet him there and ran into a friend by the train station. We ambled, discussing one of his most recent dates – *a total disaster*. I felt quietly happy, like I was in love with the world and everyone in it. As the sky dimmed to a light pink, I thought about turning to my friend and saying that we could just continue walking, but, also, I would miss everyone else.

My boyfriend arrived late, already drunk. He flopped down onto the stool I'd found for him and complained that it was wobbly. Then he got up and went to the bar, without offering to get anyone else something. I noticed my friends' glances and smiled tightly at them. I tried to rejoin the conversation we'd been having, but my mind seemed split, most of it dragged over to the bar, where my boyfriend was incensed.

When he came back, my boyfriend deliberately pushed himself out, pretending that he and the stool couldn't fit into the gap we had made for him. I persevered, but my friends quickly grew bored, and soon, my boyfriend and I were sitting silently together, while everyone else focused on other, deeper conversations. The evening's potential shattered.

As we walked to the station, my boyfriend accused my friends of being *too posh* or *intimidating*. He had nothing to say to them because they just weren't into the same things. I reasoned with him: he and I liked similar things, and I had a lot in common with my friends; what he was feeling wasn't necessarily true.

'You wouldn't know how it feels,' he said. 'You haven't been *bullied* like I have. I can tell when people don't like me.'

'You know I didn't have a nice time at school either,' I said. 'But they *do* like you.'

He was marching. I had to run to keep up with him, a little dog being led around a ring.

I continued: 'Meeting a new group of people is hard! I felt like that when I met some of your friends. I wanted them to like me.'

'My friends have always been nice to you,' he said.

'Yes!' I said, desperate now. 'You know I like all your friends. That doesn't mean I don't know how you feel.'

He stormed ahead without me, through the barriers of the train station, while I fumbled in my bag for my ticket.

I shouted after him, and people turned to stare. He disappeared down the escalators and got on a train home, leaving me on an empty platform to wait half an hour for the next one – the last one home, which was always splattered with vomit, full of people smoking.

I acquiesced and decided to feel sorry for him then. I accepted that I'd pushed too hard. I didn't want to make him uncomfortable; I *did* know what it felt like to not fit in. I stopped seeing my friends, slowly rejecting their invitations, pretending to forget to answer their texts. It felt easier that way. I reasoned that I was getting older now, too old for getting drunk at the pub or long nights out. I settled into the quietness of my life.

So I felt odd, like I was dreaming, when Eddie sat down gently on my sofa in the flat. My mind was clouded, half in my past life, half in the living room with Eddie. I boiled the kettle, even though it was much too hot for coffee, and Eddie spoke loudly over it about something work-related. I could tell he was buying time, and eyeing me carefully, to see if I would take a funny turn. I hurried around, straightening and wiping things, embarrassed by how the sofa creaked and sagged as he turned and watched. I knew he'd seen the flat in disarray when I was unwell, but its true state only now became clear to me.

I came back to the sofa, mugs steaming, the smell of the drinks like a bin that needed to be taken out. Eddie looked at me with concern.

'How are you?' he said.

'I'm really sorry for calling you out here,' I said. 'I think I just panicked.'

'Are you feeling better?'

I nodded. 'I really just don't like being unwell, you know?'

'I don't think anyone does, especially if they live alone.' Eddie took a long sip from his coffee and politely pretended that it wasn't disgusting. 'What do you think it was?'

'Probably a virus,' I said. 'I think there's something going around.'

Eddie looked dissatisfied; he studied his mug. I feigned drinking from mine. I didn't want to talk about it anymore, so I changed the subject.

'How's your mum?' I said.

'Not great,' said Eddie, sighing. 'The other day I went round and she'd left the hob on, and when I asked her about it, she couldn't remember turning it on. She's not even meant to cook – we have someone who delivers stuff for her.'

'What do you think you'll do?' I asked.

'I don't think there's anything to do,' he said. 'This is just it now.'

'No, probably not,' I said. 'But if there's anything I can help with, anything.'

Eddie looked at the corner of the room, as though something had moved there. He frowned. 'You can tell me if something's wrong.'

'I'm honestly fine,' I said.

'I'm really glad to hear that. But if you need someone to talk to.'

'Thank you.'

'I'm here whenever you need me.'

'Eddie, I'm okay.'

I returned our mugs to the kitchen. When I came back, Eddie was still looking at the corner. He turned to look at me, pulling a smile onto his face. He changed the conversation.

'I was thinking of learning to make sourdough this weekend.'

'Is sourdough as bad as kombucha?'

'Definitely not.'

'I don't know,' I said. 'They all seem like fermenting things sitting around the flat to me.'

'It could be worse. I could be getting really into baking.'

'But I like cake.'

'I tried it once and put too many eggs in some mixture and ended up with these rubbery cookies. I couldn't even bite into them,' said Eddie.

'Okay, then. Please keep your wares to yourself,' I said. 'You know, my mum always had this funny thing when baking. She insisted we smash the eggshells – really smash them.'

'I've heard of that,' said Eddie. 'It's something superstitious.'

'Like the salt and the devil? Apparently eggshell powder is good for you.'

'You can eat it?'

'No, I think to just have around,' I said, gesturing around the room.

The atmosphere settled, then. Eddie and I spoke about some other things – the newest beers he'd tried, some workplace gossip about an email that shouldn't have been sent to everyone.

'My therapist says I'm doing well,' said Eddie.

'Well done,' I said, and then wasn't sure I'd made it clear that I was being genuine.

'He says I'm handling things as best as I possibly can, under the circumstances, which is really nice to hear.'

'That's good.'

'Although I wonder where I'm meant to go from this. Like, what do you do when you know how to deal with everything, but everything is still shit?'

There was a tap at the door, the fingernails again.

'Popular,' said Eddie, as I walked to the front door.

The floorboards creaked and felt spongy, like sodden grass. I was surprised to see Jess.

'Hello,' I said, peering around the door.

'Hi!' she said.

'Did you just knock on my door?' I said, stupidly.

If Chelsea smelt of fresh earth, flowers peeking up from the soil, Jess smelt like a crisp winter morning – almost smoky, or dusty, as though she were shedding something old. She was wearing dark purple lipstick and had her nails painted a purple so deep it was almost black.

'I think you have my friend's parcel,' she said.

'Oh,' I said. 'Yes.'

Jess stuck her foot out so that the door would stay open.

'Thanks,' I said.

Eddie watched me from the sofa as I ducked into the bedroom and came out with Chelsea's clock and lighter wrapped in a plastic bag.

'I accidentally opened it,' I said to Jess.

'I'm sure that's fine,' she said, smiling. Then she lowered her voice, 'I'm glad you're feeling better.'

She turned and let herself into the Walkers' flat, which struck me as peculiar. I was sure Liz and Mark hadn't met her.

When I returned to the living room, Eddie was putting on his jacket. The zip got stuck, so his jacket was half drawn up and hung from him awkwardly.

'Who was that?' he asked.

'My neighbour's friend. Remember I said she was always having people over? I took in a parcel before I was ill.'

'Right,' he said, as if he didn't believe me.

'Are you going?'

'Hm,' said Eddie, still struggling with the zip. 'My mum, it's not good. One of the neighbours texted.'

'Oh,' I said. 'Is there anything I can do?'

Eddie slapped his arms against his sides. His jacket rippled, sounding like plastic bags.

'No, it'll be fine. Thanks.' He swung around the living room, looking for something he might have left.

'If there's anything,' I said.

There was something I was meant to do, that Eddie expected from me, but I missed my cue. As we walked, the floorboards hardened under our feet, so our steps to the door echoed. Eddie inhaled sharply, as though he had something to say, but stopped himself. He didn't turn to wave as he left. I listened to his trainers thud against the steps.

The flat seemed empty and too bright once I was left alone. The tap dripped rhythmically. I was waiting, I realised, for someone to knock on the door, or to text, or for the flat to prickle again, but it seemed subdued by Eddie's visit. I drafted a few messages to him, thanking him again, and checking in on his mother, but didn't send them. They seemed desperate. This had always been my problem with my boyfriend: if I wasn't being stubborn, I was anxious to put things right. Sycophantic pandering, baby voice, hiding behind the door frames, making myself small for him. Kissing him on the cheek when I didn't want to, like I was pressing my lips into dough.

I turned on the television for background noise and then muted it when the quiz show audience started applauding. The Walkers' flat was silent, which made me think Liz and Mark were out. I wondered, then, what Chelsea and Jess could be doing.

I looked through my peephole for any sign of them. Closer to them, I could hear their laughter – deep and rasping. Jess's smoky smell, like incense, curled under the door. The lights flared and dimmed, urging me to do something. Without giving myself time to think better of it, I unlocked the front door, went over to the Walkers' flat in my socks and tapped at the door with my fingernails.

Eight

The Walkers had opened up their flat, so the kitchen, dining room and living room were one wide space. Chelsea and Jess had covered every available surface with candles: tall and white, little pink tea lights resembling cupcakes, burned and gnarled candles inside jars, so the smoke from the wicks coiled, as if trapped behind the glass. We were sitting in candlelight only, the shadows flickering against the walls, growing and shrinking along the floor. I was surprised by the décor. I had always imagined the Walkers' flat to be cluttered and dark, a slightly less shabby version of my own. But it was bright and airy, and full of gold accents, so everything glittered and glinted. Their extensive record collection was neatly lined up on low shelves, the guitars and amps hidden away somewhere in another room or cupboard. The flat smelt of clean clothes, bleach and perfume. Car headlights from the road below flashed past every so often.

The two teenagers had opened the windows and a breeze whipped through the flat, so the candles flickered, dangerously, licking the air. There were two sofas in the middle of the room, facing each other. I was on the dark green one; Chelsea and Jess sat on the ochre one, cross-legged, and turned towards one another.

'My mum and dad are on *"date night,"'* said Chelsea, making quotation marks with her fingers.

Jess snorted, as though the concept were ridiculous. She then blinked at me, suddenly coming to terms with my age. She knew that I'd had date nights too.

'When will they be back?' I asked.

'Late,' said Chelsea.

'Plenty of time for us to *talk*,' said Jess. She and Chelsea shot glances at each other.

I wondered what I was doing – why I was in my neighbour's flat with two teenagers. I felt ridiculous, ridiculed, like they had already been making jokes at my expense. But I had seen what Chelsea and Jess could do, and thought that perhaps I was like them – trying to find meaning elsewhere, enduring everyday life. I was concerned about Chelsea, that much was true. I didn't like what I'd seen of Joseph, and the incident with the police worried me, so I reasoned that my motivations were not entirely selfish. Of course, Chelsea and Jess might find my presence odd. And if they rejected me, or tried to push me for information I did not want to share, what could two teenagers do to me, really?

'So,' said Chelsea, taking a gulp from her wine. 'What made you want to start practising?'

'It felt necessary,' I said, choosing my words carefully. I quickly changed the subject. 'What made you start all of this?'

Jess responded eagerly, 'I've always felt, like, *connected* to things. I really like being in nature, and I'm great with succulents. And then I saw this video about being a green witch, and it totally described me, so we tried some stuff. We're not sure what Chelsea is yet.'

'I didn't realise it was so complicated,' I said.

'It's not, once you get into it. We could show you,' said Jess, shooting a pointed glance at Chelsea.

'Well, I do think I was a bit ambitious. I suppose I *was* hoping you'd help me,' I said.

Chelsea and Jess looked at one another again, which meant my plan was working. But it was very girlish of them to pretend I couldn't see their glances. Subtlety comes later in life; perhaps they'd start to learn it at university, or their first real jobs.

I swilled my wine around the glass and brought my legs up onto the sofa, crossing them. The wine was cheap, almost vinegary, but I appreciated the gesture of hospitality.

Jess and Chelsea ran through my cord-cutting spell, discussing candles, the necessary items, and what I'd done wrong – ostensibly, everything.

'You shouldn't do anything you don't know how to fix,' said Chelsea, feigning authority.

'Is there something else I could try?' I asked.

'Well, it depends on what you want to do,' said Jess.

'What are you interested in?' said Chelsea.

'Banishing negative energy,' I said, repeating something I'd read on the internet.

Jess nodded solemnly.

I continued: 'But, honestly, I'm not sure how much I believe in it.'

'Why not?' said Chelsea. 'People believe in all kinds of things.'

'Like some witches think that you shouldn't hex anyone,' said Jess. 'But we don't believe that. Hexing is inherent to witchcraft.'

Chelsea rolled her eyes and mimicked, '*Inherent?*'

Jess grinned.

'Jess is going to study English at uni, and now she thinks she's a walking dictionary,' Chelsea said.

'English *Language*, which is different,' Jess said earnestly.

Chelsea continued: 'Cord-cutting works if you do it right. Or that's what I've heard. I've never had to do it. It's quite *serious.*' She looked at me inquiringly then, like she'd caught me in her hand. 'What were you trying to do?'

'Like I said, banish negative energy.'

Chelsea seemed impressed by my evasion.

'What would you use for something like the other night?' I deflected.

'What do you mean?' asked Jess.

'When the police came here,' I said.

Silence cloaked the room; the mood fluctuated quickly, like a bath that suddenly has too much cold water. Chelsea and Jess looked again at one another.

'I told you, that was nothing,' said Chelsea, her face reddening.

Jess leaned forward, studying me.

'I don't mean to pry, but I heard you arguing with your boyfriend again,' I said.

Jess sighed, and sank back into the sofa.

Chelsea blinked, and then: 'We're fine. He can be a dickhead sometimes, but that's just Joseph. He's not very considerate, you know?'

'Yeah,' said Jess.

I had to be careful about what I said next.

'Is there a spell for that?' I said. 'Like, one that could make all men not be dickheads?'

Chelsea snorted, and said, 'It would have to be fucking powerful.'

The candles flickered, almost sparking. The room felt warmer again, and I knew I'd won her over.

'Uh-huh,' said Jess, standing up. 'But we could do it.'

Swaying, she made her way to the bathroom, still holding her wine glass. Two cars raced down the road, crunching the loose bits of tarmac, like something terrible was happening far away.

'Thanks for the wine,' I said to Chelsea. 'And for helping.'

'I know what it feels like to be desperate,' Chelsea said.

'Right,' I said.

'No, I just meant – I know what it feels like to want to feel better. It's complicated. I just know what it's like to want to feel in control, you know?'

I nodded, showing I understood. Teenage girls were predisposed to drama in their speech, heightening even the most serious of situations. But at least Chelsea was trying to make her life better. I was impressed that she knew so much about her practice; she was far more serious about it than I'd imagined. I remembered what I'd been like at her age. Miserable. Prone to crying over boys, or pretending that I didn't care about them. Getting very drunk, falling over kerbs and down flights of stairs. Deliberately not eating before I went out. Hauling myself into my weekend job behind a till, eyes burning, wondering how I would make it. I was called *enigmatic*, by boys, a lot. *Independent, opinionated.*

I wanted to reassure Chelsea, and tell her that there would be more to her life than this, that in a few years she'd look back and admire her younger self. I couldn't lie and say that it would only get better from here, but at least it would be different.

'Are you sure you're okay?' I said.

She looked at me for a long time, like an animal waiting to see if it was safe to move.

'I would just like it if, you know, people were consistent,' she said. 'I don't like to be messed around. There's a lot going on at the moment – school, my mum and dad arguing all the time, Joseph. And I . . . well, I sometimes feel like I'm crazy. I'm probably not, but I'm really intuitive about a lot of things. But whenever I do something he doesn't like, it's *psycho* this and *psycho* that. And I don't think that's fair.'

'No,' I said, shifting towards the edge of my seat. 'You don't have to listen to that, though.'

'It's not just him,' she continued. 'Everyone *expects* me to be happy and, like, deal with whatever's going on.'

'No one should be allowed to make you feel that way,' I said. 'You can do what you want.'

'I know,' she said, slowly, as though thinking about what she wanted to say. 'And it will be over soon.'

'What do you mean?'

'All of this, I suppose.'

Chelsea seemed wretched, like me, and the more she avoided my questions about the incident with the police, the more I was certain of Joseph's transgressions. She must have convinced Mark and Liz it wasn't worth pressing charges, the whole thing a misunderstanding, and now she was seeing him again. Hesitantly, they'd allow it, not to lose her. It's what my parents had done.

She brightened as Jess came back in.

'We all make mistakes, though,' said Jess, somehow with a full glass of wine. 'Like the other week. I take it you know all about that?'

'I think you did something like healing?'

'That was stupid,' said Chelsea. 'But I wasn't going to do a love spell. That's *really* stupid – only new people try that. And they don't even work. But, actually, I've heard spells are meant to be better with three.' She pointed to each of us in turn to demonstrate.

'Have you been watching *Charmed* again?' scoffed Jess.

'No!' said Chelsea. 'I read it online somewhere.'

'Sure.'

Before I'd arrived, they were going to carve candles. We sat at the dining table, which was tall and made of glass, and pushed the lighted candles to one end, careful not to spill the wax.

'Carving is just another way of casting a spell,' Chelsea said. 'But it's a bit more purposeful. You burn the candle all the way down and ask it for what you want.'

I gathered that Chelsea was going to carve Joseph's name into her candle.

'It's potent. But not undoable. You just blow out the candle if you want it to stop,' said Jess. 'If you don't want to stop the spell, you have to put it out with your fingers.'

'And then light it every day until the candle is gone,' I said.

'Yeah,' said Jess, visibly impressed by my knowledge.

She turned her hands towards me, so I could see her palms. Her fingertips were scarred with raised tissue, patterned in ragged crosses. I tried not to look alarmed. I felt old, then, much bigger than them both.

Jess carved into the side of her candle with a small, sharp knife. She slipped and cut herself, and then swore loudly, sucking on her thumb.

'Is that safe?' I said.

'Yeah,' said Chelsea. 'You can't really do anything bad to someone with carving. It's more for positive things. So, for example, if you want to create a positive connection, you can put someone's name on one side and yours on the other. And you can add things. Oh!'

She got up from the table, raking the chair along the floor so that it screamed.

'Do you want a go?' said Jess, pointing her knife at me, then gesturing around at the candles with it.

'I don't think so,' I said. 'Does it really work?'

'You'll see.'

Rain had begun to pour from the sky in a deluge. Water pooled on the windowsill and dripped onto the floor, as if someone was tapping the pane. I watched the lit candles carefully, worried they'd tip over and set the flat alight.

Chelsea came back in with a vase of pink roses – the ones Joseph had given her. The petals were browning at the edges, as though they had been singed. They drooped over the edge, exhausted. She pulled the flowers by their heads from the vase and tipped the water into the sink. Somewhat aggressively, she mashed at the rose petals with the end of a rolling pin. She looked around and saw me watching.

'It just helps,' she said.

I nodded and, forgetting myself, sipped my wine. My eyes watered at the sourness. I sniffed, and watched Jess, who was carving her own name deeply into the side of her candle.

Chelsea returned to the table, fists full of shrivelled, weeping petals and slapped them onto the wax. She rubbed them into it, anointing the wax. Stray petals tumbled to the floor, landing in the puddle of rainwater.

'Ready?' said Chelsea.

'Yes,' said Jess. Her top lip had a half-moon wine stain above it.

They lit their carved candles at the same time with pink cigarette lighters. The wicks snapped and fizzed. The candles on the table were still flickering, the flames leaning over, like flowers searching for sunlight. Chelsea and Jess's faces glowed, and the flat was filled with the smell of roses slightly past their best.

They held hands, and then, leaning across the table, offered to take mine.

'Close your eyes,' said Chelsea.

Connected, I felt a surge of energy between us, a computer overheating and the fan going wild. But I felt calm, bathed in sun. Then, as Chelsea and Jess started chanting, murmuring, I felt as though I knew the words, a song I hadn't heard for several years. I slowly joined in, whispering, my voice growing louder as the pattern set in my mouth.

I felt my mind wander, and pictured the argument between Chelsea and Joseph, imagined Joseph getting into his car and driving as far away as possible, the car fading as it moved, as though it were ink. And then, I thought of my boyfriend. But as I tried to place him, I found him impossible to summon. I couldn't place him in our house, or anywhere of note. I tried putting him on a street, somewhere, anywhere, but he evaded me. His shape became indistinct, formless, vapour.

I sensed that something was wrong and opened my eyes. Chelsea's candle emitted a flare, like a cough, and then sputtered out. At the same time, half the candles were extinguished in one movement, as though we had thrown water over them. Over the sofas, a light bulb cracked and fell from the ceiling. Chelsea's skin grew pallid, dehydrated, and the shadows from the remaining candles crept across her face. Jess pulled away from me. She turned to look at Chelsea carefully. I had a feeling they were communicating silently.

'It's not meant to . . .' Chelsea said, weakly.

She was trying not to cry and hurried across the living space into the bathroom.

Jess scrambled to the floor to pick up the rose petals.

'Put these in a bowl,' she said. 'Can you get me some water. A glass of, I mean.'

I opened the cupboard doors until I found the mugs and then filled one from the tap.

Jess gulped down the water – trying to sober herself, I realised – and took the bowl of rose petals, which looked very sad, and disappeared into the bathroom, shutting the door behind her.

Steam billowed from under the bathroom door into the hallway, like someone was breathing into a cold night. With it, a strange mixture of smells: sulphur, mildew, the dull roses again. The water poured from the taps.

'Do you need anything?' I called.

Neither of them answered me. I wasn't sure if I should leave. I abruptly felt that I was being ridiculous – playing at being a child again, engaging in a fantasy. This latest episode was nothing more than the work of two girls with nothing better to do, whiling away the last few days of their adolescence.

I mopped the windowsill and floor with a tea towel and wrung it out over the sink. I returned to the dining table, wondering if I should extinguish the rest of the candles.

Jess came up behind me, putting her fingers to my forearm. Her skin was coarse and grainy, as if her fingertips were coated in ash. I felt a screech sit in my chest and swallowed it back down.

'You should try it,' she said.

I hovered my fingers over one of the burning wicks.

'How?' I said.

'Like clicking your fingers. Just imagine it going out.'

The wick fizzled under my skin. The flame produced the sensation of leaving my hand in the freezer for too long. A small amount of energy, like a flutter produced by an unexpected kiss, bloomed in my stomach. When I took my fingers away, they were flushed red, as though they were blushing.

All of a sudden, the remaining candles were extinguished, the lamps cut out, and the thrum of the flat stilled so that the running water seemed thunderous.

Jess laughed, 'Nice.'

She checked the light switches, but nothing would work.

'I think you did this,' she said.

'This building is really old. It happens to my flat all the time,' I said.

'We could do with you,' said Jess, stepping closer. 'It really would be better with three of us. Chelsea needs help right now.'

'I'm not sure I can,' I said, deciding it was time to leave.

Inside the bathroom, Chelsea turned off the taps. I could hear her gently sobbing, pulling a ream of toilet paper from the holder, then blowing her nose.

'The rain, wow,' Jess muttered dreamily, as we stepped into the hallway, which was windowless; I wasn't sure how she could hear it.

'Well,' I said, crossing to my door, wanting to be away from her.

My fingers tingled. Through the door, I heard the usual clunks and bangs from the flat. It was happy I was back, like a restless dog jumping up at the door.

Jess waited for me to go inside. I hovered, looking at her through the peephole.

'See you soon,' she called.

Inside, my flat was illuminated only by the yellow eyes of the lamp posts outside. The rooms smelt rotten – not the damp Eddie had noticed, but like a rat had crawled into the walls and died. I felt my way through to the kitchen for a glass of water, and then back into the living room, frightened that my foot would find a soft body in the pitch-black.

Then, a flash of lightning, shocking the whole room with a white light. There, on the sofa, I was sure of it, a figure.

Thunder clapped, shaking the windows. The room was

cloaked in darkness again, like someone was holding a pillow over my face. I grasped for my phone and turned on the torch, sweeping it around the room.

Everything stood completely still.

Nine

.

Then, Saturday morning. The first day of August. Sun streaming through the windows; light on my face, wherever I went, even when I closed the blinds. Dust floating through the living room. I moved warily around the flat, waiting. The flat groaning, clicking, swelling in response. The power had returned to the Walkers' flat (I could hear Liz vacuuming, Mark watching the football), but remained off in my own. I checked the fuse board, flipped all the switches back and forth, and suddenly everything came back on, purring.

I had no plans and, exhausted from the week, felt little motivation for anything. I opened Instagram on my phone, and scrolled through photos I'd seen before. I passed through profiles like a ghost, frightened that a movement – one accidental like – would reveal me to the world. I worried that my boyfriend was searching for my name and had found my reinstated profile. I knew him well. One image of a distinctive tree, the name of a shop, a telling reflection, and he'd find me. I should have made a fake account, I knew, but I hadn't thought of this when I'd first been searching for Chelsea. I told myself I wasn't doing anything wrong, or dangerous – I just had to be invisible.

There were no new posts on Chelsea's profile, which, considering the night before, made sense, but worried me. I wondered if she was okay, and what happened when a candle-carving spell went wrong. Would she be unwell, like me, and need help? I couldn't knock on the door when her parents were at home.

On Jess's profile, there was a new post, a pale pink square, with black text: *YOU WILL NEVER HAVE TO CHASE WHAT WANTS TO STAY WITH YOU.* Underneath, she'd written, *So true*, with a black heart emoji. A message for Chelsea, I thought, who had not liked or commented on the post.

Joseph had uploaded a photo of himself posing with his car, half-sitting on the bonnet. The caption: *get in loser*. I closed the tab in disgust.

In the afternoon, Mark and Liz appeared in the corridor again, facing each other, leaning up against the wall. I watched through the peephole as Liz folded her arms.

'What did you tell her?' she said.

'That we're going out for the day.'

'For God's sake.'

'It's the truth.'

'She can tell we're lying, you know.'

'I know,' Mark said. 'But I don't want to have to tell her. We should do it together, after the appointment with the person.'

'You mean *the therapist*,' said Liz.

'Yeah,' said Mark.

Liz sighed, and peeled herself away from the wall. She walked to the stairs, and Mark slowly followed.

Later, Chelsea tapped on the door. I looked at her through the peephole first. She was beaming, wearing make-up. She had curled her hair and was wearing a summer dress. Around her neck hung a large pink crystal. I reviewed my own outfit – an oversized white T-shirt, and loose, cotton shorts I sometimes slept in – and knew I should make more of an effort. When I opened the door, Chelsea placed her hands on the door frame and leaned forward, on her toes, as though beckoning me. And, in return, I felt as though there were hands on my body, tilting me towards her.

Chelsea was already retreating into the Walkers' living room, calling to Jess about almond milk. The Walkers' flat smelt sweet, like honey and jasmine; they were baking brownies, too. The chocolate smelt earthy and burned. The dining table was now covered in bowls and spoons, broken bars of chocolate and a tin of caramel. The aroma was overwhelming.

'My boyfriend is coming over,' said Chelsea, dipping her finger into a bowl of brownie batter.

'So it worked?' I asked.

'Of course it worked,' said Chelsea. 'I wanted it to, so it did. And today is going to work, too.'

'Well, everyone likes brownies,' I said, helplessly.

'Yeah,' said Jess. Her sarcasm was apparent. She leaned against the arm of the ochre sofa, her feet up on the cushions. I sat opposite her, and she uncurled slightly.

'Joseph really likes them,' Chelsea said. 'Especially salted caramel. We thought about blondies, but then, no one really eats blondies.'

'I wanted to make cookies,' said Jess, scrolling on her phone.

'Jess is waiting for someone to text her,' said Chelsea, widening her eyes.

'How long has it been?' I asked.

'Five — no, six — hours,' said Chelsea.

'He could be busy, but also, he's been online twice since then,' said Jess. 'What do you think?'

Their analysis was almost comical — I remembered doing similar things with my friends — but I understood the anxiety: waiting for someone was torturous, unpredictable. I wondered, not for the first time, what my boyfriend would think of this. Spending time with teenagers, embroiling myself in their relationships. But it was, maybe, my only chance to be without him, and for Chelsea to be without Joseph.

'Does he have a job?' I said, trying to get Jess to look at me. My voice sounded unusually high, like I was straining.

Jess frowned. 'No,' she said, finally glancing at me. 'Not like that. He works with brands — social media stuff. He's a bit older. I hate *boys*, which is why I can't wait to go to uni.'

'They're even worse there,' I said.

Jess rolled her eyes and looked miserable.

'It's probably best to distract yourself. Shall we finish these?' I pointed towards the dining-room table.

'Fine,' Jess said, getting up from the sofa. She slid across the floor in her socks, as though she were skating.

'No!' said Chelsea. 'That's not why you're here.'

Jess continued sliding around the room.

'Obviously there's a reason why you're into all this' — Chelsea gestured with a wooden spoon — 'which you can share with us when you're ready, but we thought you might like to, you know, *join in* with us, a bit more permanently.'

'Great,' I said, ignoring the invitation to share more about myself. 'What does that involve?'

Chelsea came very close to me then, her nose a few inches from mine. I wondered if her image would ripple if I touched her.

'You'll see,' she said.

'Don't worry,' said Jess, pointing to a tray of brownies. 'We'll make sure you don't get one of the spiked ones.'

Chelsea's phone hummed, and then she said, 'He's early.'

Jess and I waited quietly as Chelsea went downstairs to fetch Joseph. I thought that he must have known his way around the building by now – collecting him seemed unnecessary. The Walkers' oven began to rumble, warming up, as if it were thinking about something particularly strenuous. Jess sighed.

'Is uni really that bad?' she said.

'Oh,' I said. 'No, I'm sorry. I can be a bit, you know. You'll have a great time.'

She studied me, and then stuck her finger into the middle of a brownie.

Joseph had to stoop to fit through the door. He was wearing a light blue T-shirt I'd seen a few times on his Instagram account. It was creased, probably from being screwed up and picked up from his bedroom floor. When Chelsea introduced us, he nodded, frowning. I raised my hand in a frozen wave.

As if on cue, Jess and I moved towards the ochre sofa, while Joseph and Chelsea went into the kitchen. She pointed at another tray of brownies through the oven door, and he kissed the top of her head.

Jess typed on her phone, glaring at the screen.

'Heard anything?' I asked.

'No,' she said.

'Oh no.'

'I know,' she deadpanned.

Chelsea and Joseph came to sit down opposite us. They leaned against each other, like they would fall over without something to prop them up. I watched Joseph carefully – the way he stretched his arm along the back of the sofa, how the room felt charged with him in it, like any one of us could attack.

'Are you coming tonight?' Joseph said, looking at me.

He was trying to catch me out, I realised – he knew I was much too old to be with Chelsea and Jess. I tried not to look embarrassed, but I felt heat soaring to my neck.

'No,' said Jess. 'I have much better things to do.' She caught my eye and wiggled her fingers at me, like a witch.

'Sure,' said Joseph. 'Normally Chels can't get rid of you.'

Jess blanched, then worried at her nail varnish.

'No,' I intervened, although I had no idea what anyone was referring to.

'House party,' Chelsea said. 'Someone from the other school. Normally, we wouldn't bother with that sort of thing, because then we get caught up in the *drama* of people we don't even know. But all our friends are going.'

'Yeah,' I said.

'We have to make an appearance, you know?' said Chelsea. 'To be polite.'

'How do you two know each other?' Joseph interrupted.

Chelsea and I exchanged glances. I understood that I was to answer.

'I live next door,' I said. 'I moved in a few months ago.'

'Are you at uni?'

'No,' I said, feeling the heat rise to my face. 'I graduated a while ago. I work for an energy company. There were some problems here last night with the electricity, so Chelsea asked me to help out.'

Joseph nodded and smiled – sneered. 'Everything looks fine now.'

It was clear he didn't like or trust me. I saw it from his perspective: an older woman, suddenly in his girlfriend's flat. That could mean trouble for him.

'And what about you?' I asked.

'At sixth form.'

'And after?'

'Dunno.'

'Hm,' I said, smiling back. 'You might want to think about that.'

Jess watched me, her expression a mixture of amusement and interest. She broke the silence: 'I'm texting someone else now.'

'About time you found some other friends,' said Joseph.

Jess glared at him and tried to kick his leg. I realised I was expecting something else to happen – like sparks to shoot out of Jess's foot or hands. I listened to them go back and forth like this, Jess and Joseph throwing barbs at one another, Chelsea blinking at them in a state of bliss.

Until ten months ago, I'd known what it felt like to be protected by a relationship, to think that no matter how bad things got, at least I wasn't alone. Any time I'd thought about leaving my boyfriend, after indulging in the fantasies about where I'd live, I'd panic, wondering what my life would be like without someone else: days stretching out endlessly, cooking sad meals and portioning out the leftovers, feeling like it wasn't worth putting the heating on for one person, no one to text with my inane thoughts or little errands. I'd known – even if I didn't lose my friends – that I would feel unseen, pointless, and I'd left him, anyway. I must have tricked myself into thinking it wouldn't be so bad. But it was.

There was a lull when Jess got up to go to the bathroom. She took her phone with her, nose close to the screen as she typed. We picked at the brownies, slightly charred at the edges and undercooked in the middle. I wondered if Chelsea had turned on the grill instead of the oven.

'How did you two meet?' I asked.

'At school,' said Joseph.

'Well, actually,' said Chelsea, 'Joseph only started at sixth form. We *first* met at McDonald's, but he doesn't remember it.'

'She thinks we met as a group,' Joseph said. He moved his arm behind Chelsea, resting his hand on her shoulder oddly, hooked like talons.

'We did!' said Chelsea. 'We just didn't speak much. And then he turned up at sixth form, and he started talking to me. I was making noodles in the common-room microwave, which you're apparently not meant to do. All the girls said I should talk to him, they said I should go for it. I walked straight up to him, and I told him I knew him, kind of, and he *said* he couldn't remember me, but I think he was embarrassed.'

Joseph shook his head. 'I honestly didn't.'

'But you do now, don't you?' she said, voice pitching to a whine.

I shifted in my seat; I knew that sound. Chelsea was desperate now, needling, needing approval.

'No,' he said. 'I don't even think I remember that time in the common room. One day I looked down, and you were there.'

Chelsea laughed hollowly. Joseph and I picked some more at our brownies. Chelsea didn't touch hers, deep in thought, pulling at the split ends of her hair. I wanted to reach out to her, to calm her hands.

'Is this your own recipe?' I asked, trying to fill the silence.

'No,' Chelsea said. 'Nigella.'

Joseph snorted.

'What?' said Chelsea, shifting away from him.

I put my plate down and leaned forward.

'Come on, these are terrible,' he said.

Chelsea stayed still; I wondered if she might break in two.

'Excuse me,' I said.

Jess came back in and stopped a few paces from the door. She looked at me, then at Joseph's head. She understood what had happened; it was palpable, the split second before someone cries.

Joseph stared at me, 'It was a joke.' He turned to Chelsea, 'She knows it was a joke.'

He gave her a shove on the shoulder, which he intended to be read as playful but was much too hard. Jess moved closer, insect-fast, so that she stood behind his back. Her hands were shaking. Joseph looked around at Jess, then back to me. The brownies seemed to have clogged my mouth; my jaw felt heavy, stuck.

'Of course,' said Chelsea, finally. She whipped her head around to look at Jess, then back to me. 'I'll try again. Maybe we should make cookies next time?'

Jess placed a hand on the back of the sofa. Joseph was looking at me, laughing.

'What,' he said.

I was up on my feet now, towering over him. I pointed my finger at him, stabbing the air. 'I see you. I see what you're doing. It won't end well for you. It never ends well for people like you.'

My hiss fizzled, venomous; I was surprised at the sound, but pleased at my theatrics. I intended to frighten him and was startled at how easily I felt this rising up in me, a feeling that I could harm him – that I wanted to harm him.

'Maybe you should leave,' said Jess, looking down at the top of Joseph's head.

He looked up at her. 'No. Chels doesn't want me to, do you?'

Chelsea was looking between us, eyes darting, wide.

'It's fine,' she said. 'It's honestly fine.'

'Do Mark and Liz know you're here?' I said.

'What,' said Joseph.

Chelsea muttered my name.

'I don't think you should be here,' I said, leaning closer.

Jess moved so she was standing behind Chelsea.

'Leave it, please,' Chelsea said.

Joseph was pale now, so deeply uncomfortable I almost laughed. He wiped his hands on his jeans, avoiding my glare.

Chelsea turned and anxiously placed a hand on Jess's; the room softened, as if blurred out of focus. Jess nodded at me, and I exhaled.

Chelsea said, quietly, 'My mum and dad will be home soon.'

We all stayed in our positions, waiting for someone to move. I remained quiet, suddenly embarrassed by my outburst, at what I might have done.

Jess slowly gathered her tote bag and hovered by the door.

Turning to Chelsea, I said, 'Tell me if you need anything.'

She ducked her head, avoiding me.

I looked at Jess, 'And you.'

Joseph and Chelsea stayed in the living room; Jess and I left without further ceremony.

'Nice,' said Jess, as we stood in the corridor. 'No one ever talks to him like that.'

'I was awful,' I said. 'I really shouldn't have.'

'We could do something about it. We could help Chelsea, before he—' She paused dramatically.

'Before he what?'

'She's my best friend. I keep on thinking about what's going to happen when we go to uni.'

'You'll still be friends,' I said, gently.

She paused on the stairs and turned around, looking frightened. 'That's not what I mean at all.'

Lying in bed, I followed Chelsea and Joseph's movements at the party through their Instagram updates. Joseph teleported around the house, gathering people to him. They stood underneath his arms, as though he were shading them from harsh light. In photos with girls – none of them Chelsea – he looked at the camera, or slightly above it, communicating with the photographer. He held a bottle of beer by its neck. The girls looked down, smiling, attempting to appear candid. These were captioned with things like: *my favs* or *girls x*. In photos with other boys, Joseph was always in the middle. The other boys turned their bodies slightly towards him, arms wrapped around his back. Under one photo, Joseph wrote: *young dumb and living off mum*.

Chelsea uploaded several photos of herself, alone, and without captions. In all of them, she had a plastic cup in her hand which was full to the brim. A few minutes after she uploaded the photo, she would delete it and replace it with another. Sometimes, people were in the background, deep in conversation. In others, she had clearly hidden herself in the bathroom, using the full-length mirror to capture her outfit: tight, knee-length khaki-green dress, lace-up ankle boots, cropped black jacket, quilted cross-body bag. She covered her face with her phone.

I could visualise the events, as if I was there with Chelsea, as if these were my own memories. In her final photo, she was crying. She had taken a close-up of her face, directly looking into the camera. Her glitter eyeshadow was smeared, collecting in the corners of her eyes. Two tears had fallen symmetrically, leaving black streaks down her cheeks. She uploaded and deleted it so quickly, I thought it was a photo of my own face.

Ten

That night, a fox, yelping and glowing in the lamplight, ran across the front garden. I parted the blind to look at it and found it staring back, its face twisted as though trying not to laugh at a punishing joke. I pressed my phone against the window, hoping to get a photo of it. It came out yellowy and blurry. The fox had moved, so its face seemed even more mangled and startling.

The sky was black and almost matte, like a bin bag. I'd woken from another dream about my boyfriend, the shadowy figure chasing me through the house. This time, as it caught me at the door, I said *I know you'll be back, but you have to go now.*

The flat didn't like this. In the kitchen, the tap turned itself on and off repeatedly. On my bedside table, my glass of water was tipped over, its contents had spilled across the carpet. The glass rolled back and forth, nearly falling off the edge — a taunt, a threat. I hid under my thin sheet, hoping nothing worse would happen. 'Sorry,' I whispered.

When the flat appeared to be satisfied and stilled, I listened out for Chelsea, waiting for her to return from the party. I felt anxious about what I had done in the Walkers' flat.

I was frightened by how I had shouted at Joseph, and afraid of who I might *really* be. What if, underneath my sense that I was the victim of my boyfriend's behaviour, I had deserved it all along? What if it was *my* temper that had caused all the arguments, my rancour that had ruined everything, had borne all the bruises and misery? I picked at this thought like a scab.

I also didn't know if I had made things better or worse for Chelsea – if Joseph had now taken it all out on her, belittled by me. I knew this was likely, and cursed myself. I had never known when to leave my boyfriend alone, when to not provoke him; now, my mistakes spilled outwards, infinite, shape-shifting.

I contemplated something my mother once said: *You rarely shout, and if you do, I think, 'Oh, that's not you.'* Then, I saw myself sitting on the edge of the bed in my boyfriend's house, listening out for his return. We had been together for three years at this point. What was he angry with me for? I couldn't remember. This sometimes happened – the argument snaking and fracturing so often, I couldn't trace it back to its roots. Perhaps I'd not woken him properly again; maybe we had argued the night before. The arguments were so frequent then, the space between them closing, shifting like overcrowded teeth.

When he came home, I knew that I had changed. Instead of cooking, cleaning, handing him his dinner, ironing his shirt, I stopped trying to appease. I lay on the bed and refused to answer him, childishly. When he started picking on me, calling me *lazy, a child, stupid*, I threw myself into a rage, trying to match him. I called him everything I could think of, told him I was sick of him too. I did not leave him alone. I followed him down the stairs, unleashing a recitation of all his flaws and crimes, each one beginning with, *you always*. I did not touch him, but packed a bag hastily, as he thrashed around the kitchen, taking it out on the plates, the cupboard doors. He dented the fridge by kicking it.

When I attempted to leave, he barricaded the door and pinned me to the wall by my wrists. *I hate you,* I said, damning him. *I fucking hate you.* I repeated it until it became a scream. He seemed shocked at this: his face wrenched in pain, mine in a cruel grimace, understanding now what it felt like to win. Did I mean it? I didn't really know. But his shock, his hurt, real or not (how could I trust that anything he did was true?), felt satisfactory, like I had achieved something: I now knew how to get through to him.

Since leaving, I had been convincing myself that this monstrous version of myself was only brought out in the extreme – she, spitting, wild, was not the real me, only came out because she had to, was the response to an acute threat. But now, she had shown herself in front of others, when she was in no peril at all.

The flat let out a shuddery exhalation, and a draught moved through the room. I pulled the sheet tightly to my neck. Deep knocking came from inside the walls, as though someone were hammering. My phone lit up and cast an icy blue light across the room. It was Eddie:

Hi, are you awake?

I typed and deleted, many times before sending: *Yes.* Eddie: *I had a feeling you would be*

Mum's not well again

Sorry I haven't been around a lot, been doubling up my therapy sessions

I wrote: *I'm so sorry, I should have texted you. Why are you awake?*

Eddie: *Yeah, it's scary, but will get better*

Couldn't sleep

You?

I replied: *Same. A fox woke me up*

Eddie sent a fox emoji, and: *Anyway how are you?*

I looked around the bedroom. The flat was still again, for now. I knew I only had moments to reveal myself a little more, as if peeling back a veil.

I wrote, choosing my words carefully: *Things have been a bit stressful here. I've not really been feeling like myself . . .*

Eddie: *Yeah, work has been horrible*

I'm sorry you can't sleep

I sent him the photo of the fox, as evidence, and wrote: *I hope things will calm down a bit soon.*

Eddie typed for a long time, and stopped. Finally: *Coooool.*

I crafted the next text carefully, wanting to save myself, knowing Eddie would have the answer: *Could you recommend a therapist, actually?*

I waited for Eddie's reply, watching his status flicker from online to a timestamp, and back again. I moved around the flat, listening to it tick, my heart beating in anticipation. I went to my peephole, sensing that I wasn't the only one awake in the building. I expected the click of the Walkers' door, Chelsea to be shuffling out of her shoes. But the corridor was bathed in a darkness which shifted, like pixels moving forward and backwards, as though it were growing and swallowing mine and the Walkers' flat.

I checked the lock on the door and found it open. I twisted it quickly, trying to remember if I'd locked it when I came back, what could have distracted me to leave it unbolted. I slid the chain into place, which jangled, and I pressed my eye to the peephole. The darkness had settled down now. I waited, expecting something to move. The flat was silent. We were both breathing shallowly. I put my hand to the wall; it felt slick with a cold sweat.

I felt as though something was following me into the living room, pressing at my heels. I paused in the middle of the room, looking around, frightened of what might appear. I told myself to move, to run, to get out, but I couldn't. I knew then that I hadn't been imagining all the flat's movements and sounds. There was a presence living here with me.

Suddenly, I felt my anger flare, like a spurt of a flame. The scent of an extinguished candle filled the room. I imagined I was Chelsea, and saw a shadowy version of myself, as though she had walked into the flat and become part of me, stretching out into the areas of my body that felt tight. So much air, all of a sudden. I imagined that I wasn't really in the room anymore, not if I didn't want to be: my outline was blurred – half there, half not. I felt bigger this way, more capable, confident. Able to speak more loudly. As I expanded, as a current swept through me, I felt that this version of myself could confront the presence, potentially banish it. One last moment of malice, and then I'd go to therapy, try to be a better person.

I cracked open the part of myself where I housed all my hatred for my boyfriend, all my loathing of myself, for everything that had made my life like this. It was a stagnant smog, and I felt it smother the living room, filling the corners.

Determined now, I moved through the flat and unlocked and opened the front door. The chain clanged as though someone were rushing past. *Get out,* I spat. *Get the fuck out of my house.*

On Tuesday, Eddie drove me to my first therapy appointment. I could have walked there or caught the bus. He reasoned that I'd be tired after a day at work, and what if the bus ran late? I assumed he thought I might not attend without a chaperone. Perhaps he knew I was having second thoughts. But I accepted, hoping that this gesture would bring about a new, softer me. I had to start acting like a better person if I wanted to be one.

Each morning, when I woke, I expected to be greeted by the flat's usual disturbance. As I walked through the rooms, assessing their mood, I recognised the flat's animation as dimmer, the presence of someone else muted, almost not there. There was no scratching now, just a slight hum – though that could have just been the fridge, I acknowledged. But it was undeniable: something had changed. What if the presence was dulled by my outburst? Could it detect something new in me? I couldn't let it come back.

'We don't have to talk about it,' said Eddie, his hands tightly wound around the steering wheel.

'Thank you,' I said, looking out the window. There were dead pigeons splattered along the road, almost in a row, heads missing, guts spread along the tarmac. A seagull swooped down and then took flight, holding the corpse of a pigeon in its beak.

'I think you're really going to like it,' he smiled. 'Or, like, get something out of it.'

I was seeing a private therapist this time, reasoning that the money I was saving by not commuting to work anymore might counteract the expense. I'd transferred the money to the therapist's personal assistant that morning – a swift kick of sickness as I hit *confirm*.

The therapist was called Rob. He wore a dark grey suit, shiny black shoes, which seemed far too much for the heat. His office was the same as any other therapist's: tub chairs, pine, accents of red. The large window overlooked a central courtyard, dark and cavernous at the bottom. I sat in my chair, feeling too big for it.

'What are you here for?' said Rob.

'I think I'm stressed,' I said.

'And what's causing that stress?' Rob asked, scribbling on his notepad.

I decided I hated him.

'Work, some personal stuff.'

'Okay, then,' said Rob with a tight smile. 'We'll need to do a bit of paperwork before we can begin officially.'

I left deflated. I had forgotten (and so was annoyed at myself) that the first session of therapy was always an assessment – ticking boxes about how I felt about myself, how well I was sleeping, if I was a danger to myself or others. I lied when I answered that question about harm, knowing that the form was without nuance; if I couldn't explain myself, it was better to not tell the truth. There was not a box in which to write: *I have been casting spells with my teenage neighbour and I think I might be losing control.*

I'd told Eddie not to wait, that I'd walk home. Sun shone through the trees, dappling the pavement. The air was full of the scent of grass, its distress signal. As I walked, I reasoned that going to therapy had been an overreaction, an unnecessary step; my rage wasn't out of control. In fact, my response to Joseph, to the presence, considering everything, was actually very reasonable. And, really, I was in control of myself – I knew exactly what I was doing. I just needed a bit of help.

Maybe it was Rob's fault. He hadn't been particularly warm. I didn't see myself opening up to him, and anyway, I decided that I was fine, and everything would be fine soon. I just needed to practise the spells some more. I just needed to forget about my boyfriend.

Alice was standing on the front garden when I returned, shielding her eyes from the sun with her hand. She wore a bikini top and denim shorts. I felt embarrassed by the paleness of my legs in my yellow dress, and realised I looked like an ice lolly.

'Oh, hi!' Alice said. 'I'm waiting for a delivery. They said they'd be here ten minutes ago. Do you think they've got lost?'

'We're not exactly hard to find,' I said.

She gasped and said, 'I didn't tell you! We have a moving date – in a couple of weeks, basically.' She pulled an exaggerated sad face, her lip sticking out.

'That's really great.'

'We'll miss it here, but we're *very* excited.'

'I don't blame you,' I said. 'This place is falling apart.'

Alice looked at me quizzically.

'The fuses seem to go every other day.'

'Really?' said Alice. 'We've never had a problem with that. Maybe you should speak to your landlord? We're so *lucky* not to have one of those! They're awful, aren't they. Anyway, I'm having the new sofa delivered, that's what I'm waiting for.'

I noticed, with relief, that I didn't feel the slightest bit annoyed at Alice – just baffled.

'Why didn't you get it delivered to the new house?'

'Don't tell anyone, but the new house has *mice*.'

'Oh no,' I said.

'We had them when we first moved in here, too, and they were so difficult to get rid of. Scratching at night, making it sound like someone was living in the walls. Sean had nightmares about it. He thought we were being *haunted*.'

Eleven

It was Jess's suggestion to hex Joseph.

In her latest Instagram update, she'd posted another inspirational quote, this time against a black background: *I WISH PEOPLE COULD DRINK THEIR WORDS AND REALISE HOW BITTER THEY TASTE.* She captioned it with the skull emoji. I followed her account, and she followed me back. Then I sent her a message. I told her I had something to discuss with her. Could she meet me for coffee that Saturday afternoon? She said she was bored, of course she could.

The wind rippled through the puddles down on the street. All morning it had been raining humidly – five minutes off, five minutes on, like the world had forgotten it was upset, then started crying again. The café was practically empty, so we could hear our voices echo against the chalkboards. Jess was wearing all black, and dark, circular sunglasses, purple lipstick, a lace choker. Rings with little silver moons on them, matching earrings.

'What do we say if Chelsea sees us?' I said, looking round.

'She won't,' Jess said. 'She hates coffee.'

She leaned over the table and grabbed my wrist, then flipped my palm over. A surge of something again, like stepping onto a moving escalator. She studied my hand.

'Can you do palm reading?' I said.

Jess made a hacking sound, somewhere between a laugh and a cough. 'No, I'm looking at the burns on your fingers.'

'Nearly healed.'

'Not bad. You might be a natural.'

The waitress arrived with our coffees: black for me, while Jess ordered an elaborate Frappuccino with sprinkles and glitter. She took a photo of our cups.

'Am I in that?' I said.

'No,' Jess said defensively. 'I wasn't going to post it.'

'Okay.'

'I gathered you're funny about that kind of thing,' she said. 'Your profile is really empty.'

'I just wouldn't want Chelsea to think we'd been talking about her behind her back,' I said quickly, not wanting to reveal that I was frightened that my boyfriend would recognise my hands, figure out which café we were in and then hunt me down.

'Even though we *are* talking about her,' said Jess.

'I'm worried about her.'

'You mean Joseph?' said Jess. 'I'd probably like him if he wasn't my friend's boyfriend – if I didn't see things so closely. Everyone else thinks she's really happy, but I know she's not.'

I nodded. 'But it's toxic,' I said, knowing that was a popular label for relationships like Chelsea's. All over Instagram: *toxiiiiiic.*

132

Jess sighed, 'It's really sad, because she used to be so much more confident. She's *always* had a boyfriend, for as long as I've known her. Even when we weren't really friends, I knew who she was seeing.'

I nodded, and felt, again, that the language of teenage girls was so narrow: boys, boyfriends, falling out, school. I tried to imagine Chelsea and Jess at university, at work, and struggled. They were so young, really.

'It's good that you have each other,' I said.

Jess ran her tongue over her lips, as though thinking about something delicious, forbidden.

'I don't think she naturally fits into that group – you know, the *popular* people? She's the baby of the year, people push her around.'

'I really don't miss school at all,' I said, sympathetically.

'Sixth form is a bit different, but everyone's still got their groups.'

'It's the same in offices, I'm afraid.'

'Oh good,' said Jess. 'I can't wait to be sixty and still wonder if I'm going to be picked last for netball. Anyway, this year's been hard for Chels, that's all I'm trying to say. Everyone was really shocked when she started going out with Joseph. She's not his usual type.'

'What is his usual type?'

'Loud,' said Jess, 'Dramatic. And really into fake tan.'

She tipped some salt from a shaker onto the table and started to make patterns with it: a sun, a wonky star.

'You don't seem twenty-six,' said Jess. 'Sometimes you do, but a lot of the time you seem like us, like our age.'

I didn't know what to make of this, but I knew what

my boyfriend would say: *You child, you idiot, how sad to not have friends your own age, and even then, not really friends at all.* I tried to push my coffee cup away and spilled it over the table. The dregs dribbled out, vanishing over the edge.

Jess watched me fumble with napkins. 'Of course, Joseph thinks I'm a *terrible* influence.'

'Why?'

'Oh, he hates all this stuff' – she wiggled her fingers at me, her code – 'but mostly it's because I always figure out when he's cheated on Chels, and then I tell her. He denies it, but I've usually got proof. She ignores it, obviously.'

'I didn't know he was doing that to her,' I said quietly.

'And the rest.'

A large group came into the café then, talking over each other, pointing to tables they could push together. They looked lost, heaving suitcases up the stairs, and pushing their sunglasses on top of their heads. Their steps disturbed our cups. I had to project my voice for Jess to hear me. I sat up and looked at her directly, hoping to convey my urgency.

'Do you know what happened with the police?'

Jess looked at me steadily. I couldn't read her expression behind her glasses.

'Do you?' she said.

'I have a very good idea,' I said.

'Yeah?'

'There are bad boyfriends. It's a rite of passage, especially—' I stopped myself. 'Especially for girls. I think it's probably the only way to learn what you want, what you will and won't put up with. But I don't think Joseph is just a *bad* boyfriend. Am I right?'

Jess turned to watch the door, as though he might walk in. At the same time, the large group fell silent, averting their gazes to the walls, the plants overhead. I wondered, wanting to be convinced, if Jess had made them do that.

She whispered, 'He's really bad.'

'Does he hurt her?'

'All the time.'

'And it goes beyond cheating?'

Jess buried her head in her hands, as though she were shielding herself. She nodded gently, almost imperceptibly.

'She won't break up with him,' said Jess. 'Even her mum and dad can't get her to. They *hate* him.'

'They've said that to you?'

'Oh no, Chelsea says. But it's obvious, isn't it? That's why she and Joseph are sneaking around.'

I imagined the worst: Chelsea, unable to leave Joseph, lying in the dark in her bedroom; Joseph, cruel and calculating, telling her that it was all her fault. The relationship with Joseph would damage her, I knew, and so it had to end before it drilled right down, trapping her for ever.

'So what do we do?' I said.

'I haven't tried it before, but we could do something to keep him away from her,' Jess said. She looked up at the ceiling, in prayer. She closed her eyes and spread her hands across the table. Her mouth moved like she was chanting. I checked that no one was watching us.

I said, hoping to bring her back, 'Cord-cutting?'

'No,' she said. 'Something *for* him. She won't stay away from him. It doesn't matter what he does.' She pushed her sunglasses to the top of her head. Tears spilled from her eyes.

'Then we need to do it soon,' I said.

As the days passed, Jess sent me examples of the kind of thing she wanted to do, and what we'd need.

Jess: *do you think a dick hex actually works*
     i read scum manifesto today
     have you read it

I replied: *Yes, but I don't know how seriously you should take that*

Jess: *i know what you mean*
     it's like when chels made me watch the craft
     did you see it when it first came out???
     i just feel like until then witches were unfairly represented
     like where the fuck did the cauldron and black cat thing come from
     but have you noticed that now witches are always really skinny and beautiful
     where are the normal ones
     anyway
     FUUUUUUUCK BOYSSSSS

I wanted to say, *Yes, this is the world, it's unfair, and I'm so sorry about it.* I tried to remember if I had been this enraged at her age, this in tune with things. I couldn't remember. My life before my boyfriend seemed so small now, so indistinct. Everything before him was washed out, sodden and blurred.

I was angry at the world, too. I riled myself up thinking about Joseph, scrolling through his Instagram profile. When I saw his face, I hated him. I thought our phones might become black holes to swallow our anger, allow ourselves space to burn out. I wondered if we'd actually go through with the hex. But Jess and I fuelled one another, texting late into the night.

I mentioned, once, in a moment of clarity, concern about what Chelsea might make of this. Jess then stopped texting, which was devastating – I was concerned she'd go ahead without me. If I learned what to do to Joseph, I could do it to my boyfriend too. I texted again, drawing her back in: *On second thought I think she really needs us to do this. She won't do it for herself. Someone needs to look out for her.*

Jess: *yeeessss!!!! exactly*

Perhaps I did not wholly believe in the methods, but I was committed to the cause. Jess texted me with requests for objects, things needed to hex Joseph. I jumped up from my desk, alive with the purpose of an errand, something important beyond my little life. She sent me out for odd, unrelated things: a spool of black thread, chilli powder, a jar of red peppers. I walked to the corner shop and scanned the shelves, finding the closest thing. I ignored my work emails, searching websites for hexes, spells, something that would keep Joseph far away from Chelsea. I sent links to Jess during meetings and got to the end of the work day without really being sure how it had passed.

Jess asked me to print a photo of Joseph. We picked it together: Joseph on the beach, wearing a bucket hat and large, reflective sunglasses. He looked like a cartoon bug, pointing at the camera.

Jess: *do you think you could catch a rat*
with a trap i mean
but like leave it alive

can you buy a rat online

I wrote: *Probably, why?*

Jess: *do you really want to know????* with a crystal ball emoji.

Chelsea hid inside the Walkers' flat that week, only tiptoeing in and out to go to the corner shop with Liz. She pulled her hair back into a ponytail, and looked pale. There were dark circles under her eyes, as though her mascara had stained her skin. The flat, usually so in tune with her movements, my concerns, remained dormant. I waited by the peephole, hoping for a sign of what she was feeling. Mark and Liz always appeared to be in the flat, plugging in their amps and playing their records, so I couldn't knock on the door to check on her. In the evenings, they stood like guards outside their front door, whispering to one another.

'I can't believe you said that,' said Liz.

'We're meant to be honest,' said Mark.

'You can be honest without being mean. You don't have to go in for the kill all the time.'

'What about Chelsea? She's not coping well with everything.'

'I don't know.'

I didn't have another way to contact Chelsea. Before I could follow her account, she made her Instagram profile private, and then deactivated it. Joseph continued to upload photos from the party. There were other girls in the photos, kissing him on the cheek, holding his hand, leaning in. I knew this wasn't proof of anything, but I felt sad for Chelsea.

During this time, the world seemed agitated. The door to the block got stuck shut, expanding and contracting in the sun. I felt, lying on my bed, that it was only a matter of time until someone – something – pushed through the door and found me lying there helplessly. The flat had a constant aura of an impending visitor, but no one knocked. I tried to trust the flat's quietness. I wanted to believe I would be left alone now.

On my walks, people sped up to walk closely behind me, and then sighed impatiently when they wanted to overtake me. At pedestrian crossings, they stood at my shoulder, rather than standing at my side, and pushed past me to get ahead.

A nail technician's shop was broken into one night, the glass shimmering across the pavement and into the road. No one could contact the landlord. The shop alarm screeched down the main street and to the flat, tunnelling down the road like grief. It carried on so long and loudly that I almost grew used to it, falling asleep to its cry. But I woke up several times in the night, my legs shaking, the moon slicing through the window like a knife.

Twelve

Jess turned the radio down as I got into her car. We'd arranged to meet at the park, where Chelsea wouldn't see us. Jess had been listening to something I assumed was intended to distance her thoughts: loud, frenetic, without lyrics. Perhaps she was having doubts and wanted to ignore them.

My legs stuck to the seat after a few moments, sweat pooling at the base of my back. The heat travelled through the car so aggressively I felt like we were being boiled. The air smelt of sun cream and overripe bins.

In the reflection of Jess's sunglasses, I looked pale, small. I sat up straighter, determined to feel powerful, to allow that feeling to emanate from me into her. I had to make sure this went ahead. It wouldn't work without us both. The sunlight was low and golden, everything not touched by its light shifting into shadow. Magic hour.

'Where are we going?' I asked.

'Another park,' she said. 'It's further away. I don't want anyone I know to see us.'

Her hands stuck to the wheel as she turned a corner. She wound down the windows. As we drove along the high street, a group of boys – ones she knew, I presumed – made wanking gestures.

'Ugh,' she said. 'I can't wait to leave this place.'

'Yeah,' I said, turning to look at the boys' faces, all doughy and pug-like, not yet their fully-fledged violent selves. 'But you'll be back, won't you? For Christmas and things.'

'Oh yeah,' said Jess, nodding vigorously. 'And Chels said we can book a girls' holiday. Obviously, she's going to visit me, and I'll visit her. But I think it will be different, like, better.'

'Have you heard from her?' I asked. It had been a week since the party, and I hadn't seen more than a glimpse of Chelsea.

'Not for *days*,' said Jess. 'No one's seen Joseph either. He's been hanging out with people from the other sixth form. I think they're living in the same halls at uni. Apparently, he got an unconditional offer to Aberystwyth, so he says he didn't really bother with exams, revision, whatever. But I *heard* he actually showed up to every single one.'

'He told me he didn't have any plans,' I said.

'Classic manipulation. Everyone says he's actually quite clever.'

'Really,' I said.

'I don't take any of the subjects he does,' said Jess. 'Or didn't,' she added, reminding herself to use the past tense now. There was a glimmer of pride in her voice, as though she had survived something dangerous. She continued: 'I don't like to hang around for the post-mortem.'

We pulled into a rough patch of land, which must have been the car park. Jess abandoned the car impractically, probably blocking someone's way in or out. It was still light outside, just – the sky glowing red, like a fresh graze. I felt first-date-nervous, jittery, energy igniting through my hands.

'Do you have all the stuff?' Jess said.

'Yes.'

'Did you see that one about *blinding* him?'

'That was ridiculous,' I laughed.

'Like, it *could* be possible, with the right things. But using a Ken doll? People are so stupid. It's not that hard to make a proper voodoo doll.'

'Right, very early *Buffy*,' I said.

'I've been meaning to watch it. As if wrapping toilet paper around a doll's eyes would actually blind someone! Gouging the eyes, though, that could work.'

'I don't think we should do that.'

'Yeah. But I really do want to do a spitting curse on Joseph, though.'

'You can do that if we don't get this right,' I said.

She looked at me seriously. 'We're going to get this right.'

'Of course we are.'

We worked quickly, under the cover of the trees. We chose a spot far away from other people, their screams and shouts occasionally ringing across the park. There were scorch marks dotted on the grass from campfires, like crop circles. The wind carried the smoke of cigarettes and the burning of sausages grilled on barbecues. We lined up our objects: black thread, black candle, photograph of Joseph, a knife to carve the candle.

The breeze picked up, blowing our hair across our faces.

'Can you feel that? It means we're disturbing his negative energy,' whispered Jess.

When I looked at her, I believed it. She looked powerful, untouchable, and I wanted to believe that I would be too, if I did this and it worked. I felt intoxicated, giddy with my potential, our potential.

After I had carved Joseph's name raggedly into the candle – *On both sides*, Jess told me, *so we definitely get him* – I wrapped the printed photo around it, Joseph facing outwards, and secured it with the black thread. Jess sheltered her lighter with her hand and then, when we were sure we were ready, tipped the flame onto the wick. A crack, twine splitting, and then: heat, like pleasure rising through the body.

We chanted a spell I'd printed off. Jess read it aloud first, and I mimicked, a fraction behind, until the words felt as though they were coming from deep inside me, inside my stomach, swirling into the backs of my legs, my feet, my eyes. I felt, in spite of the rhyme, despite that I would have felt embarrassed for anyone to hear us, that I had never said something more true, more important. Soon, we were in unison, a chorus, and I forgot everything around us.

When I got home, a fly whirred around the light bulb hanging in the hallway. The flat rang with its buzz. I kicked off my shoes and gazed up at it, wondering how to make it leave. It crawled round and round the bulb, as though mocking me, begging me to swat it and break something instead. I felt exhausted from the evening's spell, the energy it had taken to protect Chelsea, but I also felt accomplished, nearly at peace. I could right things if I tried, I told myself. I had the power to do that.

I moved into the kitchen, looking for something to hit the fly with, or to guide it to a window to be let out. I could hear its wings fluttering down the hallway, its legs pattering over the light fixture. I leaned down to the drawer where I kept the tea towels and felt, all of a sudden, something at my back. A rotting smell, like unbrushed teeth. I stayed still, a chill travelling through my body so quickly I felt rooted to the spot, pushed down into the floor.

A draught flew through the room, knocking the utensil pot over with a clatter. The kitchen door slammed shut, shaking the flat, and the lights went off, plunging the room into darkness. I fumbled for something on the kitchen side – the kettle, in the end – and brandished it against the intruder. But when I turned, the room was empty, except for me. Suddenly, it was unbearably humid. The kitchen smelt like melting tarmac. Sweat trickled down my arm.

I wasted very little time. I set myself up in the bathroom. This spell would be different, I told myself. I was different, now. I did it in complete darkness, no longer apprehensive, and led only by what I could feel, what I could sense. When my fingers found the candle or lighter, they sparked with an affirming shock. I completed the ritual again by memory, by instinct, like I had done it many times before. The candlelight danced across the tiles in its own ceremony, encouraging me. Once I was chanting, that pleasant heat crept through my body. Slower, deeper, this time, as though I was being thoroughly cleaned. Breath at my neck, like someone was holding me until I fell asleep.

When I opened my eyes, it was morning, and the flat was completely, utterly still.

The news reported, incorrectly, that as August reached its midpoint, people would need their jumpers again. Instead, the embers of the summer heat reignited. I squinted at my computer screen for a few hours, before deciding to clock off early. I made the most of the patches of sun on the front lawn, keeping my distance from the neighbours' children, who kicked their footballs towards the windows, or sprayed anyone in their vicinity with water guns. I drifted in and out of sleep out there, dreamlessly, forehead printed into the grass.

I avoided Eddie. Since the disappointment of the first therapy session, I hadn't booked a second, and ignored Rob's personal assistant's emails. Eddie had texted after the first appointment, asking if I was okay, and then again, coincidentally, right after I'd been with Jess. Eddie's name flashed across my screen in emails sent to all employees. I looked to see if he was still there, still emailing. It occurred to me every time that he was probably looking for my name too, making sure I was still alive, waiting for my response.

I was embarrassed by having asked for his help, irritated with him for making me think therapy might be the solution. And how could I, in good faith, return to the therapist's room when I knew I had no intention of trying to make it work? What I could do with Jess, with Chelsea, and by myself now, felt exciting, commanding, loud – not vengeful, I told myself, but empowering. There was no solution in therapy, I felt – just worksheets and tick boxes and revealing the worst of myself over and over, to no avail.

And the flat had been peaceful, calm, for days. Before, I had felt like I was living in the stomach of some awful creature, swallowed whole and tortured by its rumblings, its movements and whims. But now that I had cast the spell, I felt like I had crawled out and could see where I lived for the first time. I set to improving things, buying cushions, place mats, blankets, candles for every room. If I left the flat for a walk, I knew that when I came back, everything would be in its position; I knew I would be safe.

I did not have another nightmare. The presence that had chased me in my dreams vanished, the confrontation settled. When I woke, I felt well-rested, listening to the pigeons cooing, the jolt of a fly trying and failing to come through the window.

I texted Jess: *I think it worked.*

Jess: *yeah i think so*
i haven't heard from chels
have you???

I hadn't heard much movement in the Walkers' flat. Occasionally, the sound of Mark dropping something heavy, then swearing, or Liz shouting his name until he said, *What?* back. Where was Chelsea? I assumed that now the summer was drawing to an end, she'd be celebrating her final days before leaving for university. I expected the sound of her wobbling down the stairs in heels, or coming back late, shuffling along the wall to the front door. I lay on the front lawn hoping to catch her, convincing myself that I hadn't imagined her. But I didn't hear her, much less see her, for two weeks.

I texted Jess: *Has she gone on holiday?*

Jess: *i'd know if she'd done that*

I typed: *Maybe she's broken up with him? Maybe she's really*
upset. Should we check on her?

Jess: *leave her*
  i'll find out

My life slipped into stillness. I kept my routines and tried
to worry less about Chelsea. I wanted to believe the spell had
worked. Chelsea's silence must be proof of it – if she had
broken up with Joseph, wouldn't she be crying, recovering?
Wouldn't she be roping Jess and I into more failed spells?
I knew Jess would get through to her. It was just teenage
drama, after all. I had the more serious problems in life. I
had to look after this quietness, now. I would protect it at
all costs.

Alice and Sean moved out of the block the next Tuesday,
their foreheads dripping with sweat as they loaded boxes
into the van they'd hired. I'd spread an old sheet across the
front lawn to sunbathe, and scrolled on my phone, hoping
they wouldn't ask me to help.

'Oh my god,' Alice shouted over to me. 'I thought we
could do it ourselves, but we really should have got a man
with the van.'

I offered her my bottle of water, which she drained
completely. Sean was hiding behind some boxes, so he
didn't have to speak to me.

'Don't worry. My parents are driving over,' Alice said.
'They're really helpful. Sean's parents live too far away, but
they bought us the sofa.'

'Did they find you eventually?' I said.

'Oh, you were right! We got it sent to the new house after all. I'm going to miss your advice! You're just so practical.'

Sean dropped something inside the van and yelped.

'Look,' Alice said. 'Here's my number. I know you said you don't do social media. When we've moved in properly, I'd love to have you over.'

I smiled at this, sincerely.

Alice turned as the bass line of a dance song stemmed from the top of the road. An engine revved obnoxiously. Then, so quickly I told myself I must have been imagining it: Joseph's car, racing past us, windows down. I strained to look for Chelsea in the passenger seat. I told myself she wouldn't be there. She couldn't be.

Thirteen

I should have known things were nearly over when my boyfriend began harming me in public. On a hike, we walked into some dense woods – to get out of the sun, I thought, to explore the area. In the cool shade, our skin was speckled with light. We mopped our foreheads with the bottoms of our T-shirts. I said something small about how hot it was, and he replied that I had embarrassed him in front of his friends the other night. Couldn't I just behave? Why did I have to answer in detail when asked about our plans? Why couldn't I leave that alone? I didn't know, in truth. I suppose I should have stopped myself from being honest, from making a quip about waiting for him to propose. I'd made him look ridiculous.

In retrospect, my obsession with waiting for him to propose was silly. In the moments I wasn't convinced that I had doomed us, I fixated on getting married, sure that this would repair everything. I thought that tying him to me would mean that everything I had endured, the test, had been worth it. The solution to my ambivalence would be commitment, I thought – *his* commitment, too. I had long worried I wouldn't be able to commit to anyone, but here I was, years later – no wandering eye, living with someone, willing to stay even when I wanted to leave. In the calmer moments, the days between an argument, I reasoned that I wasn't bored with my boyfriend. I liked my life when it was going well. When it wasn't, I assumed everyone was experiencing the same, or would do at some point. I knew people argued, compromised – what I had gone through was an elevated version of it, that was all.

But we were too young – me, especially – to be thinking of marriage. And the reason I thought of it so much (and not children, which we argued about constantly, each of us willing and then reluctant in turn) was because I thought he might, finally, make his way to anger management therapy. It was my latest appeal after every incident. I thought, naively, that marriage meant respect, so no more belittling, beating. I thought it would mean that he loved me.

When we returned to the path to continue our walk, I made things worse. I asked too often if he wanted a drink, or something to eat. Then I stopped talking in case I said the wrong thing. Then, forgetting myself, I offered him sun cream for his burning nose.

We made it to the car park, full of people packing up picnics, bundling their children and dogs into their seats. I was aware of people turning to watch us, my boyfriend stalking ahead, me tripping to keep up with him. I hoped I could make things better before we started driving. I stood behind him and put my hand on his shoulder, leaning forward to kiss his cheek, even though he was sweaty, and his skin filled my mouth with salt. He reached up, slowly, to hold my hand, I thought. But then he held my wrist, tightening his grip, and twisting. Pain flared, as though he was searing my skin. *You're hurting me*, I might have said. If I did, no one intervened.

In the car, on the way home, all was forgiven. The air conditioning was broken, so we rolled down the windows and sucked noisily on ice lollies. I gripped our finished sticks and wrappers in my hand, and fell asleep with my head tipped back.

When I woke up, half an hour later, I asked to put on some music. The sun was going down now, golden light engulfing the car. Once, we had been sitting in our garden, sharing some stories from our weeks. The light had been just like this – heavy, burning – and he'd stopped me mid-sentence to say, *You just look so beautiful.*

The car bounced along the motorway. My boyfriend had wound the windows up so I could sleep, he said. He apologised for finishing our bottle of water. When he was like this, I loved him so much I didn't know what to do. I knew I'd die for him, however dramatic that felt to recognise, or state to myself. I looked at him and felt like crying.

I opened his phone to find something to listen to. On the home screen: notifications of messages from a woman, a name I didn't recognise. We were allowed to unlock each other's phones, and to read the other's messages aloud. We trusted each other. If there was something to hide, he'd be cleverer than this.

'She says she wants to see that band with you,' I said, trying not to put my palm to my chest, where I was sure my heart was visibly beating.

He didn't respond.

★

A week later, we met a group of my boyfriend's friends in a pub garden. We trapped wasps in glasses, so they'd stop bothering us, promising that we'd release them once it was time to go home. The light was slipping away, but it was warm enough that all our arms were bare, flushing with sunburn or glowing with tan, depending on what we'd been doing earlier in the day. I was making my best efforts to be the version of me he loved: independent, funny, good with his friends. I wanted them to be my friends too, so I asked a lot of questions.

'So are you from here?' I said to two women, squashed together on the other side of the picnic bench. They seemed lovely – all smiles, lipstick and denim jackets and long hair.

'Ah yeah, always lived close by,' one of them said, 'but we work in the city centre. Becky originally said she was going to move to London, but this was cheaper. Get to live with your parents rent-free, don't you, Beck?'

'I work in marketing,' said Becky, rolling her eyes. 'I really didn't plan on being back here, but now I am. And I kind of like it. Or tolerate it, I don't know.'

The first woman nodded. 'It's definitely cheaper, and, like, everyone *thinks* they're going to go to London after uni, but it's shit.'

Becky said. 'Have you ever noticed that when you blow your nose after being in London, it comes out black? Awful.'

'Did you live there for a bit?' I asked.

'Oh fuck no!' the first woman said. 'Weekends only, like, twice a year maximum. I get too tired of it, and it's so expensive. Too many fucking people, too fucking big. No family down there either, which is another fucking requirement of life in London.'

'Sasha,' Becky paused and looked at her friend, helping me out, 'is training to be a teacher. Can you believe it?'

'I wasted two years working in a pub saving to travel, then decided I didn't want to do it alone, and I wasn't joining one of those groups. And then thought, *How can I make meaning in my life?* By having twelve-year-olds calling me a bitch, apparently,' said Sasha.

I laughed, loudly, my laugh reserved for when I felt totally relaxed.

'I work in energy,' I said. 'Mostly because on Fridays they let you drink wine at your desk.'

'I think my job would be one-thousand per cent easier if I could drink,' said Sasha. She took a sip of her cider. 'Little shits.'

'Energy,' said Becky. 'Is that fun?'

I took a long, dramatic pause.

'No,' I said.

We all laughed.

My boyfriend glanced at me from across the beer garden, smiling. I warmed with something like comfort to know that it was all going to be okay now. I was a good girlfriend; I could get it right. He hadn't stayed late at work all week.

We moved, at some point, to a bar where we could dance. My boyfriend had always said I was a good dancer; it was the first thing he noticed about me. Sometimes, late at night, when we both couldn't sleep, he'd admit that he couldn't actually remember the beginning of our relationship. *You remember so much,* he said. *I can't even remember what I thought of you.* I'd comfort him, pretending that this hadn't stung. *It matters that we're here now,* I'd say, willing myself to believe it.

That night, my boyfriend avoided me on the dance floor, surrounded by his friends. He stopped looking at me and, even when a song we both loved came on, turned his body away from mine, so that it felt like we were strangers, and I had to chase him all over again.

Becky and Sasha, drunk and now in love with one another, forgot about me, screaming, *Oh my god!* any time the DJ stopped the track before the best part. I waited for them to invite me to the toilets with them, or the smoking area, but they just smiled at me, or, once, pushed me towards my boyfriend, as though I was shy and needed encouragement. I danced on the periphery of the circle; it was too late, too loud, to try to make friends now. The lights pulsed in sickly blues and pinks. I could feel the music vibrate in my chest. I was independent, I reminded myself. We needn't be, together all the time.

One of my boyfriend's friends, a tall man whose name I didn't remember, leaned down and said something into my ear.

I leaned back and said, 'What?'

He tried again.

I pulled back and nodded. I said, 'Yeah,' and smiled, hoping this would make him leave me alone.

He put his hand to my arm, and I shifted, slightly, so that his fingers hung in a small gap between us. I said my boyfriend's name, loudly, like it was a badge, and the man danced away from me. I knew I should have shaken my head, and said no – that would have looked better. I wondered if my boyfriend had sent him over to test me, to see whether I'd tell him all about it later. I would; I was obedient.

I caught my boyfriend looking then, mirroring me, hands slipping from some other woman's waist. The gesture could be platonic, I reminded myself, before I could get upset. Sometimes it was just platonic. It's what men did when they wanted to guide women out of the way.

I began to make trips back and forth to the toilets alone, where I could calm myself. There was no need to panic; the night didn't have to end in an argument. I tried to feel drunk again but had sobered up. My skin felt sore to touch. I walked around, alone, and bought weak shots from the sticky bar and felt nothing. I sat down for a while, until I thought that if I danced enough, I could convince myself I was having fun. I just had to make it through the night, then everything would be fine.

The bar was emptying, and the group was deciding if they wanted to carry on or not. I didn't offer an opinion. Becky and Sasha left without saying goodbye.

'They do that,' someone said when I asked about them. 'Always way too pissed. They'll fall asleep on a bench or something.'

I made a final trip to the toilets. One of my boyfriend's friends was leaning into the mirror over the sinks, applying bright red lipstick. The toilet cubicles seemed blurry, and the music pounded through the walls. There was toilet paper, sodden, stuck to the walls. Maybe I was drunk, after all.

I joined the woman at the mirror and smiled at my own reflection.

'Hi,' I said.

'Hi,' she said, smiling once she recognised me.

I dusted a generous amount of powder over my nose and checked my face. My eyes were bloodshot. The powder was a shade too light for my tan. I rubbed it in with my fingers.

'Are you having a good night?' the girl said, fluffing her hair up.

'Yes!' I said, still looking at my reflection. 'I like everyone here. Everyone is so nice. I love your top.'

The girl balanced against the sink. She slid her feet in and out of her shoes, stretching her toes.

'I really want to go home,' she said. 'But he wants to stay out.'

I said I'd see what my boyfriend wanted to do.

'How long have you been together?' she asked.

I pretended to calculate.

'Just over four years,' I said.

'I've been with mine for a year and a half.'

'Are you happy?'

'Yes,' she said, smiling. Her tongue was dyed red from cheap shots. She continued: 'I really am. I didn't think I would be, because I'm a bit of a commitment-phobe, but he's my best friend.'

I nodded emphatically, wanting to show that I understood. We were the same. We had the same thing.

'But, like, being happy isn't constant, is it,' she said.

I looked at her, smiling plainly, hoping I looked stupid,

blissfully unaware of her meaning. I didn't want her to see my panic.

'You wonder what it would be like to be without him.'

Why didn't I leave him? *You can always come back*, my mother said. It frightened me how much she knew without me telling her. I told my parents that everything was fine. We were just stressed, under pressure at work, worrying about money. Yes, I knew they could help, but I didn't think *he* would like it. Really, things would be fine soon. They always ended up being fine.

There were practical things: I'd have to find somewhere to live. His long absences gave me time to look for one-bedroom flats, to see what I could get for the car (not much). I couldn't afford anything, and ended my searches; then, a few days later, started them up again. But I wasn't thinking straight – I looked for flats in our area, and forgot to do my searches in incognito mode, neglecting to think that he might check my search history. *See*, I said to myself. *You can't really want to leave, or you'd have thought of this.*

I felt things weren't bad enough for other forms of help: the police, refuges. And, anyway, I knew from colleagues that the police were not going to intervene. One of the women from the office had disappeared for a few weeks, and I'd overheard whispers of her boyfriend having punched her while drunk. She had a black eye. When she'd called the police, they had said, *Call us if he does it again, and we'll come over*. Tuts. Sad, shaking heads. Mugs gripped with both hands. I didn't have children, which was what really warranted going to a refuge, and ultimately, beyond my stubbornness, I had somewhere to go. Plus, I reminded myself, things weren't really that bad. *I* didn't have a black eye; my bruises were always somewhere else, almost incidental. I would have left if things were really that awful. I was being dramatic; it was just another rough patch. It was usual to go through these things.

And wasn't I to blame for some of it? I knew how to anger him further in an argument, goading him. I knew that my threats to leave – which I expressed sparingly, but strategically, venomously – wounded him. I knew he was frightened of being abandoned. Hadn't I, once, so bereft at his treatment of me, told him that I wasn't sure if I could love him anymore, so that he punched the wall so hard he bled? Hadn't I then lied, and said I hadn't meant it, and then nursed him with warm water and antiseptic gel? Didn't I then promise to always love him, even as I was sure it couldn't be true? I was as bad as him, or worse.

These fantasies about leaving scared me. I found myself splitting in two, as though I could see my current self and this dangerous, unpredictable future self, the one who was going to abandon everything. I looked in the mirror and wondered if my face had always been this way – it was like meeting someone for the first time, and acknowledging, without judgement, the shape of their nose, the alignment of their teeth.

Perhaps it was silly to think I wouldn't know who I was without him. I hadn't known that before him, so it wouldn't make much difference. I thought about returning to my parents' house, their relief at my reappearance. I could see they wouldn't understand how devastated I was; they'd tell me I was away from him now, as if that could solve everything. When I imagined it, I felt an overwhelming sense of stagnation, retrograde. I knew that whatever I did, I had to keep on moving, and it had to be forward, into the dark stretch of whatever came next.

Fourteen

White clouds smuggled the sun into the penultimate week of August. When the clouds parted, splodges of blue sky appeared, like a friend stretching out their arms. I opened the windows in the morning, desperate to breathe something other than the damp musk that had settled into the flat.

I texted Jess: *I don't think it worked. I saw them together.*

She took a while to reply, getting day-drunk in huge groups at the park, lazing around in friends' gardens, updating her Instagram profile constantly. She had, at one point, incessantly texted me her inane thoughts (she texted me in the middle of the night, once: *Is 'revose' a word?*) and admitted that she was bored with everyone, could not wait to leave and start a new life at university. She worried about Chelsea, though – *she* wasn't good with change.

Jess: *i haven't heard from her*
i've tried everything
i'm trying not to spiral though
sometimes when you cast a spell it's not immediate

Chelsea and Joseph would break up at the end of summer – or, at the very latest, at Christmas break. That felt inevitable.

But I'd thought the hex was meant to end things immediately, curtail their back and forth, the torture of it, and end any possibility of future reconciliation. Had the spell even worked? I thought not, and wondered about what might happen to Chelsea, and then, of course, me. At night, I panicked, unable to sleep for fear that the flat would come alive again, and find some way to torment me. What if the presence was planning to come back stronger, more terrible? What if I had called my boyfriend to me, instead of expelling him, all his wrath and cruelty only moments away? I expected a knock on the door, something to come hurtling through the window, someone to appear behind me in the mirror.

Then, the weather changed: for two days, the rain, unceasing, crashed against pavements and flooded the road so that the water rose over the tops of my trainers and stained my socks brown. People waded along the main road, hoods up, trousers darkened from the thighs down to the tops of their shoes. They breathed heavily, as though they could blow the water away. I listened for the rustling of Chelsea's umbrella, her disgusted sigh as she kicked off her trainers and returned to the Walkers' flat, but heard nothing. She evaded me, and my sense of dread grew.

I finally spoke to her on the Wednesday afternoon, as she returned from a last-minute open day at her first-choice university. Her skirt, tight against her legs, curled up at the front. She had scabs on her knees. I had waited on the front garden for hours, sitting on a blanket, huddling against the breeze, the dull sky, enduring the stares of our neighbours, their mistrustful glances.

Chelsea stopped when she saw me and took her head-phones out.

'Hi,' she said, flatly.

We walked up the street to the café, side-by-side, the wind pushing our hair back from our faces. The weather had cooled considerably. Although it was no longer raining, the roads were flooded. The windows of the nail shop had now been boarded up. Some teenage boys, younger than Chelsea, wearing dark jackets and hats, had thrown their bikes across the pavement. They were graffitiing the boards in perfect replicas of cartoon characters, artistic versions of their names in pale blue and yellow. They sang along to a song ringing tinnily from one of their phones. We pretended not to see them.

The warmth of the café rushed to our faces as soon as we entered. We were both rosy as we slid onto benches. The window seat again. Outside, the clouds thickened, plunging us into a shadowy grey light. I asked Chelsea how she'd been – in a way, I realised, that must have signalled that I had something to tell her, or something to anticipate. She stirred her hot chocolate slowly, coating the spoon in froth.

'Terrible,' she said, dramatically. 'My parents are unbear-able. I can't live with them anymore, which is a good thing, really. They think I don't know, but it's obvious. They're just waiting for me to move out to make it official. And things with Joseph are falling apart. I think he's ready to give up.'

'What happened?' I asked, pretending I didn't know.

'I love him,' she said. 'But he's such a dick. Sometimes I try to remember if I've always been this miserable, and then he does something that makes me feel like I'll die without him. I feel like if we could just get away from everyone else, we'd be fine. It's everyone else causing the problems. I need him, especially right now.'

I tried to hide my horror. I hoped the hex would have done more than to make Chelsea even more melodramatic and dependent, lovestruck. Perhaps she just needed a push, a slight gesture towards the right path. Maybe we were meant to guide each other. I felt – despite my better judgement, knowing that it would sound ridiculous to anyone else – that we had met for a reason. I desperately needed to correct the course she was taking.

I chose my words carefully: 'I think when people are attached like you and Joseph are, they can, at times, know how to bring out the worst in each other.'

Chelsea slammed her mug down. Globs of chocolate froth splattered across the table.

'What do you want me to say?' she hissed. 'I know we'll probably break up. He got an unconditional offer from Aberystwyth, and, whatever happens, I'm going as far north as possible. I have to get away from my mum and dad. Everyone says it's hard to make a long-distance relationship work. Maybe we won't last. But what if we do?'

'It happens,' I said, trying to sound sympathetic.

'I know,' she said. 'Loads of people meet at school and stay together.'

'Of course. Or you take some time apart and get back together later.'

'Yeah.'

'Or lots of people don't, and you just learn from it, I suppose.'

'What am I meant to learn from all of this?' she said.

I thought about it.

'Something,' I said.

Chelsea sniffed. She looked as though she was trying not to cry.

My tea was too hot to drink. My palms were clammy. I now had proof that the hex hadn't worked, which meant the one I'd cast against my boyfriend hadn't either. I tried to keep my voice even.

'You can't keep on with Joseph this way,' I said.

'But you and Jess only know about the bad parts,' she said. 'I only really ever talk to Jess about Joseph when I've argued with him. She doesn't want to hear about how great things are. She says it makes her feel sick. I know I shouldn't say this, but I think she *likes* hearing about when it's gone wrong. I can't talk to my mum about him unless he's being a dickhead, because my mum hates boys and men right now – even though she pretends she doesn't – and my dad's obviously just horrified that I have a boyfriend, or he's out at the pub. My mum is always like, *Dump him!* which is really hypocritical when I think about it, *and* I don't think that's actually a solution.'

'Jess and I can help you,' I said, sounding desperate now. 'You don't have to put up with it.'

'Hm,' said Chelsea. She pushed her cup across the table. The spoon clinked against the side. 'Sometimes I have this dream. I have to look after a dog, and the dog loves people but hates other dogs. He will literally eat another dog if I let him. So, when I look after him, I have to rent a field for an hour or so a week. It's meant to be this gated space, and they text me a code to enter. I'm meant to be alone in it, so the dog can run around. We've been running around for a while, and we go into some trees. Something makes me look back, and then I realise there are other dogs in the field. I don't know how, but the dog hasn't realised yet. I have a few seconds, really, before he notices and starts to fight them. So I sit down on top of him and hold his jaws shut. The other dogs come over, and they're sniffing around him, and I think he's going to kill them if he gets away. He's growling and struggling underneath me. My legs feel sore. I scream for someone to help me. I scream like I'm dying. And no one comes.'

I thought of the house I shared with my boyfriend, and how, through the walls, I could hear our neighbours' washing machine, one of them sneezing. No one came for me, either.

'Please let us help you,' I said.

'You don't understand,' said Chelsea, looking out the window. 'I'm the dog.'

Fifteen

That Sunday, the sky was as blue and flat as a child's painting. It was unbearably hot, one final blast of heat as the summer burned out. Every surface seemed to radiate warmth. I changed my T-shirt twice, sweat pooling on my chest and lower back. A heat rash speckled my wrists. I threw open the windows and listened to the neighbours make idle talk about what a 'scorcher' it was. I heard the children on the street screaming, being sprayed by a hose.

I was lying on the sofa, cooling myself with my battery-powered handheld fan, which uselessly sputtered at my forehead. I listened out for Chelsea, who had disappeared again after our conversation. I knew, from studying Jess's Instagram, that there was going to be a big school leavers' party. Surely Chelsea would attend, and Joseph. They must have received their results by now, I realised. There had been no cheers or hugs or crying from the Walkers' flat – so what had happened to Chelsea? I hadn't seen her since our coffee, and her Instagram profile was still missing.

I thought about intervening again. What would make this better – another hex for Joseph, one for my boyfriend, or perhaps a protection spell for Chelsea, for me?

I felt utterly exhausted. I supposed this was how my boyfriend always prevailed during our push-and-pull, why it took me so long to leave: I was always drained, and distracted with trying to keep him happy, so couldn't see a way out. Now, as I had been then, I was depleted by trying to hold onto things, not let them spiral out of control. As I scrolled through Jess and Joseph's profiles, my boyfriend's voice rang in my ear: *Obsessing over children*, he'd say. *What is wrong with you?* I whispered back, irritated: *You're right, you're right. Leave me alone.*

As though I'd summoned it to me, I heard footsteps overhead. I sensed a metallic smell and taste, like blood in my mouth. The sound travelled through the walls, thundered down into the floorboards and came towards me, under the sofa. Scratching from underneath, clawing at me. I tucked my legs to my body, certain that something was going to crawl from under there and grab my ankle. The flat came back to life: scraping from the walls, a pulsing beat from a terrified heart. Then, like a hand clapped over a screaming mouth, the cries were muffled. A power cut shot through the flat, silencing the buzz of electricity.

I waited for something to happen, my pulse in my ears like someone at the door, and, when I thought it might be safest to move, leaped from the sofa and didn't look back. I ran down to the basement where the electricity meters were kept and saw that mine was clocking as usual. I checked the fuse board, and nothing seemed amiss. I breathed heavily, hoping no one would find me down by the bins, among the rats and rubbish bags torn open.

Eventually, I knew I had to return. I crept back up the stairs, wishing for a weapon, something that would save me. I edged the door open, but the flat no longer seemed disturbed. I moved methodically, slowly, through the flat, silencing the parts of myself that wanted to scream. Nothing moved.

I told myself that the problem was practical and had a logical solution. Calmed by the flat's silence, I changed plugs, removed sockets to check the wiring, called the network distributor to see if it was a regional problem (there were no reported issues). I knew to open the fridge and freezer as little as possible to preserve the low temperatures, but as the hours passed, puddles appeared on the kitchen floor. I worked quickly, telling myself there was nothing to fear, but prickled at any movement or sound in the block. I had banished my boyfriend; I had *felt* it work. He couldn't be coming for me.

Then, ringing like an alarm. Ringing like the side of my head being hit. Through the windows, huge black flies, round and full as blueberries – too many for me to stop, swat or catch. They swarmed me, crawling over my feet and arms as I tried to bat them away. Teeming into the folds of my ears, into my hair. Landing on the sofa, scuttling up the walls.

I ran to the bathroom, where I could lock myself inside. The flies stopped abruptly at the threshold, as though there were a barrier, buzzing against the space as though it were glass. I lay down on the tiles, breathing heavily.

Eddie answered on the second ring. 'Hello?' He sounded as though he were moving something heavy.

'This isn't a good time, is it?'

'No, it's fine,' he said.

'I can call back later.'

Eddie said my name sharply.

His tone surprised me; he sounded like my boyfriend. His disdain was apparent. But some part of me had expected it, truthfully. What else did I deserve? I knew myself to be irritating, grating, unlikeable. And I'd been ignoring him. What was happening in the flat was my punishment, and Eddie had seen through me.

I burst into tears. I hadn't expected to do this, hadn't felt it welling up. I wiped my eyes with the back of my hand and apologised effusively.

Eddie softened, and coaxed me, 'It's fine, honestly.'

'There's something really wrong with the flat,' I said.

'What is it?'

I explained the problems. Before I'd finished, Eddie was promising to get into his car, to help me once he'd seen his mother. Could I wait an hour? I said I could. When we hung up, I cried some more. The flies continued to drone outside the bathroom, thumping their bodies against the door.

I calmed myself and returned to the internet. I googled *spell + power cut* and *spell + electricity,* but nothing useful came up, not even from the witches selling magic stones. I scrolled through YouTube videos and settled on one in which young women practised pyrokinesis: candles snuffed out with their minds, flames lured to flare with a whistle.

Feeling brave, I crept out of the bathroom, dodging the flies, and gathered the few candles I had remaining in the flat: dusty white tea lights and the human skeleton, which had barely any wax left. I intended to fix this situation, somehow. I could make my life better; I had done it before. I knew hiding was not the solution.

I arranged the candles in a circle on the living-room floor, and, sitting cross-legged in the middle of them, set them alight. The flies hovered close to my head and crawled along the sofa. I steadied myself, trying not to flinch as they landed on me. I closed my eyes and thought of the electricity running through the wires, the crackle of the hob as it warmed up, a light bulb blinking awake.

I opened my eyes as my phone rang.

'Is your intercom working? I've been down here for a while,' said Eddie.

He came into the flat with a small can of insect repellent and a bottle of water. The flat exhaled as though it were annoyed. Its menace shrank so that it no longer felt like there was something evil in the rooms. I looked around and saw the flat as it was. Walls and floors and objects, all completely normal, except for an infestation.

'I thought you were exaggerating,' he said, batting the flies away.

I led him into the living room to show him the extent of the issue. I supposed I might have tried to put away the candles, tidied away my failed ritual. I tried to think of a logical explanation, but I was exhausted.

Eddie skirted the candles and looked at the oven, the fridge, my lamp, several of the sockets, doing what I had done – checking that everything looked as it should.

'I checked that already,' I said, cross with him, with myself. Why had I called him over if I didn't want his help?

Eddie declared that we should close the windows to prevent any more flies coming in, and shut all the doors to trap them in one room. We also needed more bug spray, some new fuses and perhaps a torch, in case the repair was beyond us and I had to live in the dark for a while. I hoped he was joking.

In the car, Eddie switched the air conditioning on. The hairs on my arms stood on end.

'Do you have the number for an electrician?' he said.

'No. I haven't needed one before. Maybe I should call my landlord.'

'It's Sunday,' said Eddie. 'He won't do anything.'

He was right, of course, but that didn't stop me feeling that he was being smug.

'I'll give you the number of someone I know,' he continued. 'Even if you don't need it this time, it's always good to have an electrician on call.'

'Thanks,' I said.

The sun spilled over my legs. I pulled my sunglasses down from the top of my head, my eyes streaming from the light. I realised I'd missed a thick strip of hair on my calf and ran my fingers across it, worrying about how noticeable it was. Eddie turned on Radio 4, and I tuned out.

Summer, two years into our relationship. It was a long bank holiday weekend, and I hadn't left the house. I lay in patches of dying sunlight, waiting for my boyfriend to come home (drunk and irritable) from seeing his friends, pretending I chose to stay in the confines of our walls, our small garden, rather than being terrified to leave, afraid of what people might see in me if I ventured out without him. In the final hours of the weekend, I suggested to my boyfriend that we go to the supermarket, prepare our lunches and dinners for the week ahead. He grunted in agreement.

In the car, he was sullen, silent. This always meant that trouble was brewing. I ran through all my possible transgressions, big or small: having not washed the plates properly; looking at my phone when we watched TV; requesting he do the vacuuming earlier in the week, because I hated it, which interrupted his time off in the evenings; asking him to talk to me about our sex life, because he hadn't fucked me for a month and I was worried that he no longer loved me.

I pressed the button to wind down our windows, and he immediately stabbed the button on his side to wind it back up.

'Are you okay?' I said.

This was possibly the tenth time I had asked that afternoon. I knew something terrible was going to happen, had sensed it since we had woken and he had flung his arm at me when I had tried to wake him with a gentle kiss. I knew that asking this, repeatedly, was only going to make things worse – each utterance a sharp flick to the forehead. It was going to make it happen faster, though, and wasn't that a relief, to have it start properly, and not hang over us all day? The sooner it happened, the sooner it could reach its conclusion, and the cycle could begin again.

'Yes,' my boyfriend seethed. 'For the millionth time, yes. What's wrong with you.'

'Nothing,' I said. 'You just don't seem very happy.'

We pulled into the heavily populated car park: parents with wide pushchairs, low sunbeams glinting on glasses, children in neon-coloured hats, smeared with dregs of sun cream. I watched, alarmed, wanting to get out among them, but found myself paralysed. I pressed the button and sealed the windows.

'You've got to stop this,' he said.

'Sorry,' I said.

He turned his head to look out the window.

'Let's just have a nice day,' I said, trying to stop my eyes from watering.

'I don't want to do this,' he said.

'What?'

'I'm not going to go in there with you and pretend everything's okay.'

'Please?' I said, palms sweating. I took the keys out of the ignition to show I was ready to go, ready to put this behind us. 'I promise I'll stop.'

He snatched the keys from me, dragging them across my hand, scoring the skin. Before I could turn my head to follow him, he had somehow exited the car, and slammed his door. The car shook. In front, a woman was heaving plastic bags into her car. She turned to me, open-mouthed.

I shouted my boyfriend's name, frightened to move, for someone to witness this further, knowing that getting out to plead with him would make me look hysterical. And then he punched the passenger window. I held my breath, waiting for the glass to shatter, but nothing happened. Everything remained eerily intact.

He was oblivious to the woman in front, who had ducked her head and was walking hurriedly to return her shopping trolley, almost running, away from me, away from us.

He stared at me and, without emotion, pressed the car key, locking me in.

I had no water, no air. The temperature rose, and I wondered if I was going to die. I couldn't bang on the window, or scream for help – that would mean someone would call the police, and then I'd have to admit what had happened, and then something terrible could happen to my boyfriend, or he could convince them (of course he would) that I was the unstable one. And then we'd have to break up; there would be no coming back from that.

I locked and unlocked my phone, thinking of someone to text or call. I didn't know how I would explain this. I panicked, crying, hyperventilating, reasoning that he had to come back eventually; he wouldn't just throw me out without at least letting me collect my things. He respected me more than that.

But I also knew that there was no turning back from this. His anger had exploded beyond our bedroom, living room, into public. I knew it didn't matter what I did – stay at home, go outside, talk to no one – I was always going to make him angry, because I was frustrating, annoying, needy. Now he'd take it out on me everywhere; there was nowhere to hide.

He returned, what felt like hours later, flushed, his forehead beading with sweat. He unlocked the car and got in, handed me the keys and told me to drive home.

★

I was shaking by the time Eddie pulled into the retail park, heading for the hardware shop and gardening centre. I was startled by how vivid my memories of my boyfriend were becoming again, as if one of the flies had crawled into my skull and laid eggs there. I had to stop it; I had to get control of my life again.

Eddie circled the car park several times, looking for an empty spot, and finally abandoned the car in a too-small space, half up the bank. People flowed out the automatic doors, pushing trolleys of compost, plant pots and saplings.

Inside, I shivered against the chill of the air conditioning. I followed Eddie around with my arms crossed over my chest and felt lost inside the endless rows of tools, door handles, light fixtures, hammers. I tried to shake the memory of my boyfriend, as though it were following me.

'What do you think?' said Eddie, showing me two different kinds of bug spray. Both had huge wasps on the front, keeled over, legs up in the air cartoonishly.

'I've never used bug spray before. Is there something else we can use?'

'Not really,' he said. 'This will do it.'

I gazed down the aisle at a large display of candles, lime green and yellow, arranged in a pyramid of terracotta pots.

'Citronella?' I said. 'Isn't that a repellent?'

'I don't think that will work,' said Eddie.

'I don't like hurting things. I don't want to.'

He placed the cans back on the shelf and looked at me sternly. 'Can I ask you something?' he said.

I nodded, heart racing, expecting the worst. My boyfriend had liked to pick arguments in the aisles of shops, not bothered if anyone could hear us. It was evident Eddie didn't really know what or how to ask and was hoping I'd fill in the gap for him.

'You sounded really upset on the phone. It's fine, it's just – you really haven't seemed yourself lately. Is something going on?'

'I'm fine,' I said. 'Honestly. It's just been a weird week at work, and then this.'

'I don't think you are, though,' said Eddie.

'Can we talk about this in the car?' I said.

I walked down the aisle and picked up two of the candles. Eddie stayed by the bug spray, pretending to read the labels on the cans. He chose four – two of each – and sidled up to me.

'Sorry,' he said. 'I shouldn't have been so pushy.'

'It's fine,' I said. 'Let's just get what we need.'

Back in the car, I was determined to be in a better mood. I rolled down my window, pleased to feel the wind whipping through my hair. Out of the flat, out in the world, sometimes I felt alive – like I'd suddenly been woken up from a nightmare and could see how beautiful everything truly was. Eddie put on some music, and we sang along, my heart trilling, but, eventually, I thought about what we might find at the flat and berated myself: I must have slipped up again – the flies could only be my fault.

Eddie turned the music down.

'So,' he said, rubbing the bridge of his nose. 'The candles?'

I pretended to watch something at the side of the road. 'Sorry?'

'The candles in your flat.'

'Something a friend showed me,' I said.

'I didn't know you had other friends,' said Eddie. It was clearly a joke, but it still stung.

Eddie turned a corner, his hands sweeping the steering wheel. Calming noise, almost sea-like.

'Is it, like, *witchy*?' he said. 'That doesn't seem very you.'

He had a point.

'Can we talk about something else?' I said.

Eddie blinked at the windscreen, concentrating on something ahead of us, a lorry swerving across two lanes. He hit the button for the hazard lights and slowed the car. We drove the rest of the way in silence, Eddie leaning forward over the steering wheel, looking for other threats.

When we returned to the flat, all the lights were on. The flies had died, bodies shrivelled like raisins. Their wings glittered. I'd only intended for my spell to bring back the electricity; I felt devastated, personally responsible for so many deaths. The flat was quiet, but perhaps it was imitating stillness, like a person pretending to be asleep.

Eddie vacuumed up the flies, seeing that I felt squeamish. As I watched him go back and forth over the same patch, I realised it made him feel heroic, or useful, as did – I assumed – most of his interactions with me. This explained his preoccupation with me, and was, of course, the sum of our friendship: he wanted to save me. And I, silly, helpless, all too willing, called him any time there was a hint of trouble. Wasn't the point of knowing Chelsea and Jess, following what they were doing, to look after myself? I wanted Eddie out of the flat then.

He walked around, flicking the light switches, opening and shutting the fridge door to ensure it was back to normal.

'I think it's working!' I called to him, but he persisted.

I shut my eyes and willed him to leave. I imagined him gathering his things, reporting that we might as well return what we had bought, if I had time tomorrow? Me making a non-committal noise. His small wave as he disappeared through the door. My relief at being alone again.

His phone rang. It was an emergency.

Sixteen

The next day, Monday, I thought I would text Eddie. It was always the thing I was going to do – after I'd sent an email, after I'd had some lunch, after I had finished my work, after I'd thought about dinner, and ate a handful of crisps instead (the salt stung my fingers, and I licked at them like I was sucking meat off a bone). I knew it could be simple; I could just ask him about his mother – how was she? But every time I picked up my phone, it felt heavy and dangerous. It was possible that I was making things worse in my imagination, but I felt I was responsible, somehow, for his mother's fall, her subsequent hospital admission.

That night, I lay awake, listening for the presence, which had not yet reared its head again. Every creak or movement in the block might have been a threat but turned out to be nothing. I knew to be alert. I reasoned that my spells, the hexes against Joseph and my boyfriend, had called some malicious presence back to me. I must have done something wrong, and angered it, waking it from its exile. Perhaps I was meddling with something that I didn't, and couldn't, understand, something much stronger than me.

On Tuesday, the sky threatened rain, thunderous clouds jaundiced and drooping. I took my daily walk, scanning the main street for Chelsea or Jess. I wondered if they could sense what had happened with my failed spells, the curse of flies. I heard nothing from them, and suddenly felt exposed, alone in the world again. The counter inside the fish and chip shop glinted as I walked past, and the smell of grease burst through the door. I smoothed my hair down, using the window to check I was still clean. Across the road, men shouted to each other, slamming their car doors. I felt light-headed, like my shoes were too heavy. I shuffled along the pavement, stopping when someone tried to pass me, or couples refused to walk in single file. I shuddered against the wind, biting and unseasonal, and tried to wrap my jacket closer.

But there was another explanation I was coming to terms with, and began to use to keep my anxiety at bay: none of this was real, and could be explained away quite easily. The spells had proven to be ineffective, and my trust in them was waning significantly. I had failed to protect Chelsea from Joseph, unsuccessfully attempted to keep the presence out of my flat, and all my efforts to forget about my boyfriend had been futile. I reasoned that Eddie's mother's fall was just an unfortunate, terrible inevitability – one caused by my neediness, by his being away to look after me, certainly. But perhaps I had not willed it into being.

Yet I still failed to reach out to Eddie, who hadn't provided an update since he'd arrived at the hospital. Every time I thought about him, I felt a pang of guilt, or dread, which I filed away somewhere until the next time it popped up, like someone waiting behind the door for me to enter the room.

When we first lived together, my boyfriend had a nasty habit of waiting for me in the corner of the living room, down the side of the sofa. If I came in late, he'd stay there, in the darkness, watching me quietly slip my coat and shoes off, using my fingers to balance against the wall. He'd wait until I was downing a glass of water in desperate gulps so it ran down my chin. Then, slowly, he'd announce himself, crawling out from the space, almost sliding across the floor, and unfold himself in front of me, head rolling up last. I'd scream, a sort of garbled gasp and low moan. I'd remember it later with a sense of shame, thinking, *What was that?* My boyfriend didn't react, and then would turn, without saying anything, and walk up the stairs to bed.

The next morning, we'd stayed under the duvet, neither of us wanting to get up to make coffee for the other.

'Why would you do that?' I said.

'What?' he said.

'Scare me like that. You know I don't like it.'

'You used to be fun,' he said, looking at the ceiling.

'I am fun,' I replied, trying to keep my voice even. 'I've just been stressed. I'll try harder.'

My boyfriend blinked.

I heard my voice pitch higher. I was trying to be girly for him. He liked that. 'Just some other games, please. I don't like that one.'

There was a game where one of us would try to climb on top of the other, and then, before the other could stop it, we'd try to stick our tongues in each other's ears, or sometimes, nostrils. I straddled my boyfriend and placed my hands either side of his head. Usually, he would play along.

Typically, he would win. But this morning, he gazed at my chin, and then gripped my arms and flipped me over, so I fell to the floor, landing on my coccyx. My shoulder crunched as I rolled it back into place. I stayed down and tried to stop myself from crying.

'I was trying to talk to you,' he said.

'I'm sorry,' I said. It came out as a whimper.

But there was no interrupting him now. He said I was a child. I had no concept of an apology. I didn't ever listen to him. I thought I could solve everything with a kiss, or sex. There was something wrong with me. There was something very wrong with me. He didn't think he could cope with me. He was trying to inject some fun into our lives. Why didn't I appreciate that. There I was, going out. He was just pleased to see me. And I had ruined it. I made him feel like he couldn't be himself. I wouldn't understand that.

This would go on for hours; when he was like this, he was unstoppable. There was a prepared stream of accusations, delivered with hatred. Sometimes I protested, other times I waited for it to be over, thinking about getting out of my pyjamas and having a shower. We could waste a whole day on this, only surfacing when it had turned dark and we suddenly found ourselves ravenous. On a few occasions, the worst ones, disgusted with myself and him, I threw some things into a bag and tried to make it to the front door.

'See,' he'd say. 'You can't even have an argument properly.'

Eventually, he stopped waiting for me in the dark when I began to expect it and checked down the side of the sofa as soon as I walked in. The surprise was gone, its effect muted. He sulked for a few days after, and then we didn't speak of it again.

When I thought about it, back then, I wondered if he was right. I was always, in some form, trying to leave. I was very eager to pack a bag and get away from him. When left alone for long periods, I knew that the relationship wouldn't last. I couldn't see its future. What did that say about my sense of commitment, my resilience? I was dooming us. I had sometimes believed that I was mean. He was just trying to play with me, and I had been insensitive about his efforts. It was true, I was becoming less fun. But, really, I knew it was nothing like that. His nasty trick was intended to disturb me, to make the house, and him, seem unpredictable. He wanted me to know that I couldn't take my safety for granted. He had wanted to make me feel unstable, and I had let him.

And suppose none of this was real – the spells and hexes, the bangs and creaks in the night – wasn't I allowing him to continue, enabling him to haunt me after all this time? If I wanted my life back, if I wanted to be better, I would have to try something else.

I came back from another walk to the corner shop on the Thursday. My flimsy carrier bag was damp with sweat, and the ends of my hair were matted. Jess was going into the Walkers' flat. Their front door stayed open. I couldn't be sure if Mark and Liz were in, so I stood on my doormat for longer than usual, pretending to struggle with my keys and the door.

Chelsea's voice echoed through the Walkers' flat, and into the corridor: 'You can come in.'

Inside the Walkers' flat, Chelsea and Jess were on the sofas, facing each other. Jess was looking at Chelsea, away from me; she didn't turn to acknowledge me. There were several black candles on the floor in between them. They had been burning for some time; thick drops of wax ran down the sides. The room smelt awful, like something had rotted. I looked around the room. Along the windowsills: black tea lights, glinting like gems.

'Come in,' Chelsea said, gesturing for me to sit beside her.

'Where are your mum and dad?' I asked, perching on the edge of the sofa. I felt ridiculous before I'd finished the sentence.

'Out,' she said, looking at Jess.

Jess tucked her chin to her chest, as though rolling herself into a ball. I could sense she was tired, perhaps regretful. I wondered if she and Chelsea had been arguing before I arrived. I could feel the row hanging like a ghoul. I knew Jess had probably told Chelsea about the hex, in some way – she wouldn't be able to keep a secret, especially from her best friend. They didn't work like that.

I shivered as my hair moved across my shoulders, like someone had touched it. I tried to sense what Chelsea was feeling. I usually felt able to understand her, her emotions a kaleidoscope of familiar patterns. But now she eluded me. She sat still, refusing to give anything away. I realised I would have to begin.

'How's everything?' I said.

Neither Chelsea nor Jess responded. They looked at each other. I took a deep breath and tried again.

'I've been having some trouble with some of this,' I said, wiggling my fingers, using Jess's code. 'Has everything been working for you?'

'*I* haven't been practising,' said Chelsea. 'What about you, Jess?'

Jess shook her head, and then mumbled, 'It hasn't been working for me.'

'What have you been doing?' asked Chelsea, turning sharply to look in my direction.

'Banishing negative energy,' I said. 'Quite a lot of it.'

'Listen,' said Chelsea. 'I know that you think it's okay to cast spells without us because you think you're more mature or whatever.' Her voice became infected with a whine. 'But we're meant to do things as a three.'

'I didn't realise it was a rule,' I said.

'That was the *point*, remember? The three of us together – it's meant to make us stronger.'

I tried to remain patient, wearied now of her melodrama, her self-centredness.

'I didn't know,' I said. 'And I don't really know what you mean by *stronger*.'

She grew exasperated: 'The point is that you didn't tell me. I let you in here, taught you things, and now you're using them against me.'

'Sorry?' I said.

Jess looked at me deliberately, signalling that she expected me to take the blame for what we had done. I had, I supposed, driven events, made sure they had happened. I thought Jess might have at least felt sorry for me, and regretful that it had turned out this way. But I knew she would save herself – this was the way of the teenage girl.

'What did you do to me and Joseph?' Chelsea said.

'I didn't do anything to you. But with him, I've had good reason. I wanted to help you.'

Chelsea paused. She closed her eyes and pressed her fingernails into her palms. I expected, as I had done so many times, to feel her anger somewhere in my body, to feel a connection to her – but it was broken. I couldn't feel anything but myself, pulsing like a flame.

'Chelsea, doesn't he hurt you?'

'Sometimes,' she said. 'But it's not bad. We just argue a lot.'

'Even if it's not physical, it counts.'

'I don't know what you're talking about,' she said, looking between me and Jess. Jess was hunched over further now, her arms wrapped around her legs. She would not look at either of us.

'At the beginning of summer, when the police officer brought you home? That was because of him, wasn't it?' I pressed.

'Oh my god, no,' said Chelsea. 'That was *nothing* to do with Joseph. I got caught drinking on the street. I didn't have my ID with me, and they thought I was lying about being eighteen. When I argued with them, they said I was too drunk, so they brought me home. My mum was livid, but I didn't get in trouble with the police – just told not to do it again, like I was some child.'

'You just said he hurt you. Jess said he hurt you,' I countered.

'Yeah, like, he's mean sometimes, doesn't think about me. He's cheated on me before, but he doesn't do that now,' said Chelsea. 'What do you think happened?'

'How is he mean to you?' I said.

'What?'

'Because there's a difference between someone being inconsiderate, or a bit of dick, and someone deliberately making you miserable. Does he control you? Tell you when you should or shouldn't go out, what to wear? Does he make you feel stupid? Does he blame you for everything? Does he try to keep you away from your friends?' I sounded desperate.

'No,' said Chelsea, quietly.

'Really?' I said. 'Because I can think of times when he's done some of those things.'

'Yeah, like, once or twice,' said Chelsea. 'But I'm just as bad. Sometimes it *is* my fault that we argue.'

I was breathing heavily now, like I'd been woken by something falling over. 'Chelsea, what he's doing to you is abusive. You don't have to put up with that.'

'No,' said Chelsea. 'He isn't. I promise you he isn't.'

'Jess told me. She told me how bad it is. I'm really sorry that he's doing this to you. But you don't have to live like this. You really, really don't.'

Chelsea was now staring at Jess. Jess had her head bent down to us, so her parting appeared like a crack of light in the dark.

'What did you say to her?' Chelsea said to Jess.

'I'm sorry,' said Jess, her voice muffled. 'I just didn't know what else to do. He's horrible to you. I'm sure you think he loves you, but he doesn't love you enough.'

'Bullshit,' said Chelsea. 'You know what I think. I think you're so jealous, you told *her* that he was abusing me.'

My heart thudded up my throat like something determined to find vengeance. I recast the events of the summer
and saw them clearly: hexing Joseph hadn't been about
knowing he and Chelsea shouldn't be together; it had been
about Jess keeping her best friend to herself. There had been
arguments, behaviour that Chelsea would one day see as
unacceptable, but perhaps it was true: Joseph was not like
my boyfriend.

'What do either of you know about relationships anyway?'
Chelsea said, turning to face me. 'You've lived here for
ages and the only boy you're ever with is that tall one,
and it's obvious you don't like him, even though he's in
love with you.'

'Do you really want to know,' I said, angry now.

Chelsea and Jess winced, as though I had wounded them.
I had thought about how I would broach this subject with
friends many times. In my imagined versions, I told people
who loved me and would not judge me. I would speak
obliquely and eloquently about what had happened to me,
what my boyfriend had done. I would be able to articulate,
within a few sentences, the terror I'd known, and, simulta-
neously, my own culpability – my understanding that even
though I wasn't to blame, I somehow *was* to blame. But
now the time had arrived, and I hadn't prepared.

'My boyfriend was abusive,' I said. 'Both emotionally and
physically. I had to escape him.'

Jess covered her face with her hands and groaned. Chelsea
blinked, as though she were struggling to understand.

'I'll never know what was real or not; it's impossible to
tell. I think it was all a lie, and then I can spend hours with

something wonderful that happened, pulling it apart until it's all just threads and a pile of nothing. It feels like I'm haunting myself.' I paused, struggling to breathe properly. I swallowed.

When Jess looked up at me, her face was flushed, and her eyes were streaming. Chelsea had a hand clasped over her mouth, her knees pulled up to her chest. Her eyes were closed. Once, I might have thought she was casting a spell.

'So if I can explain myself,' I said. 'I've been looking for a reason to live, to carry on, and I can't find it. Some days I'm certain I died in that house with him. And if I didn't, then everything I cared about or believed in died anyway. I became someone else in that house, and I hate him for that, and I hate myself. I didn't want that for you, Chelsea.'

Outside, cars thundered down the road in a sheet of white noise. We listened for some moments. I felt numb; I felt nothing.

Jess spoke first: 'I'm sorry. I had no idea. I wouldn't have—'

'It's fine,' I said.

Chelsea ran her hands through her hair. 'I'm sorry that happened. But for me it's not like that.'

'No, maybe it's not, but still,' I said. 'Joseph isn't good for you. I know that sounds ridiculous to you right now, but he's bad. Not totally, maybe, but *for you*. Or you are for each other. You can't keep on doing this to yourself.'

Chelsea uncurled and leaned towards Jess. 'What did you do to him?' she said, her eyes wide with recognition.

'We bound him, but that's it,' said Jess, wiping the tears from her face.

'Oh, fuck off,' Chelsea said. 'Seriously. What's wrong with you? You said *she'd* just been fucking around, doing weird stuff, not hexing my boyfriend!'

'If I'm being honest,' I said, 'I don't think any of it worked.'

'That's not the fucking point,' said Chelsea.

We sat quietly, then, considering what had been revealed. I knew I was too old for this – the dramatics, the fraught friendships, the bickering, which Chelsea and Jess would inevitably get over in a few days. I knew I'd had arguments like this with my friends as a teenager – everything felt so life-and-death then, so important.

And none of this would help or save me. I couldn't deny that the rituals, the binding, the hexes were point-less, futile. I did not – could not – believe in them. In following Chelsea and Jess all summer, I had exposed myself to all kinds of terrorisations, real or imagined, all manner of terrible thoughts, perpetuating my problems for myself. And for what? For this? To play witches with teenage girls who couldn't possibly understand what I had been through, who – I hoped – would never understand?

I observed them, waiting for the moment when I could slip away. I felt twice my size now, too big and old for the Walkers' flat, to be hanging out with Chelsea and Jess. As the candles became shorter, the room seemed smaller. I listened to Chelsea's and Jess's voices growing softer, their friendship being stitched back together, slightly weaker than before. My cheeks were hot, but my hands felt cold. I clenched and unclenched my hands, like I was coming back into my body after a long time away.

Seventeen

Although I had been preparing for it in many ways, leaving took me by surprise. It was early September, a few months after our fourth anniversary, the chill of autumn a whisper in the evening air; the grass, the leaves, the insects all drowsy and languishing, preparing for a long and deep sleep. My boyfriend's absences became protracted: long evenings at the office, working on a vague project; suddenly, drinks with work colleagues he'd not mentioned before. He returned home in the evenings and went straight to the bathroom, where I heard his aim falter, and his vomit splatter onto the floor, down the side of the bath. One night, a Wednesday, he fell asleep across our bed while I fetched him water, and I – too exhausted to argue further – slept downstairs.

When we were late for work the next morning, eyes bloodshot and sore to open, he accused me of sabotage.

'Why didn't you wake me up?' he spat.

'Do you think I want to be late too?' I said.

'You *know* I said I needed to be in early this week.'

'I am not your personal assistant,' I said, feeling overly formal, ludicrous.

For this, he smashed his hand through my mirror – a vintage, wooden thing my parents had bought. As I tried to run to the front door, he tore my shirt from my back, rivulets in my arms where the fabric had dug in. On my lunch break, I trawled the shops looking for the exact replica of the shirt, hoping that replacing it would remove the incident from memory, but knowing that every time I washed it and hung it out to dry, I'd think of this, and recognise the shirt as a fake, an impostor.

That night, he came home late again, in the early hours, smelling strange, unfamiliar. I blinked in the darkness, recognising the smell, its meaning. I had chosen to sleep on the sofa again in case he came home drunk once more; I couldn't face another argument. This was a mistake. He had the aura of having done something wrong, and my body, curled against the cushions, was an accusation.

'You think I'm out of control, don't you?' he said. 'You're blaming me for something I haven't done. You can't forgive me, ever, can you? You're punishing me.'

'No,' I said. 'I just know how much you need to sleep. I was listening when you said you needed this week to go well. I was doing this for you. I love you, I'm sorry.'

As I cried underneath my blanket, he shouted: 'You taste fucking disgusting, *sour*, and I don't want you anywhere near me. Want to know why I haven't fucked you recently? You *disgust* me. You wonder why I'm like this, don't you? You believe I'm awful, but really it's your fault. You don't want me to have any friends, you think everything bad that happens to you is my fault. You're fucking *insane* and everyone knows it.' He went upstairs, punching the walls.

I breathed, trying to slow down, trying to stifle my weeping. I hoped that he had passed out, would be calmer in the morning. Then I could ask him where he'd been. He'd lie, of course – but I'd know.

Without warning, he was above me, peering through the blanket.

He hissed, 'I don't think you should live here anymore.'

Then, quiet. He was not loving, but, for the next week, appeared to be revaluating his behaviour. He came home on time, or early. He didn't complain about the house, or me. In fact, it felt like we were housemates; we acknowledged one another if we happened to be in the same room, but often shut ourselves away, avoiding each other. I planned repairs and improvements – to the walls, to my appearance, to my demeanour. On my lunch breaks, I bought new dresses, underwear. I showered in the evenings, as well as the mornings, to make him want me.

I saw, now, that it was all a ruse on his part; everything was calculated. The next Friday, minutes before I was supposed to leave for work, he said he was visiting friends for the weekend. He was playing with his hair in the mirror, pulling at large chunks with his fingers. He hadn't packed a bag and grew irritated when I queried this. Where was he going? When would he be back? How were they travelling? Their route didn't make sense. What were they going to do? How long had he been planning this?

'Shut up,' he said.

I followed him downstairs, pleading with the back of his shirt, translucent with sweat. Then, somehow, moments or hours later, he pushed me into the living room, onto the floor, and I stayed down, hoping as I heard the front door slam that he would call me later to ask what was for dinner, to say he'd made a mistake and he was going away next weekend, actually, or – I prayed – not at all.

But he switched his phone off, so I couldn't contact him. I wailed around the house, damning it with my grief. Sunday evening came and passed. I lay awake until Monday, the daylight, like greying milk, leaking through the windows. My panic grew in me invasively – I couldn't think straight, drafted texts to my mum, asking for help.

I called in sick to work, and lay at the top of the stairs, praying for his return. I knew it, then. I knew this was the end. If he came back, he was coming back to me ultimately changed, unrecognisable. I knew what he was doing, where he was, and felt sick, like something terrible was living inside me. I hadn't been enough, couldn't ever be enough. I had pushed him away with all my pleading and fawning. Perhaps I might have saved things if I had looked after myself. I saw myself from a remove: greasy hair, no make-up, baggy clothes; disgusting. If I'd just *behaved*.

In a moment of weakness, of shame, I turned on his laptop and searched through everything I could find: photos he hadn't shown me, though nothing I could use as ultimately incriminating – group shots of people I'd never met, his arms around strangers; his emails, of which there was nothing unusual, although I noticed that he had deactivated all of mine to him; he had, he said, deleted all his social media accounts, but I found them under a fake name – crawling with a secret life in which he'd cut me out. I appeared nowhere, couldn't find a trace of myself, as though I didn't exist.

And then, on an email account I didn't know about, and in an inbox I didn't know he'd created, I found them: hundreds of emails between him and someone else, and before that, him and someone else, and before that, shortly, someone else, and so on. He must have thought emails would be easier to hide. I howled, unhuman, and felt myself break in two. In one email, someone wrote: *Don't you have a girlfriend?*

I moved through the house with precision and determination. I did not know when he would come back and would not be confronted by him. I had stayed all along in the belief that what I endured was the price to pay for being loved, that it was all worth it to have him as mine, to know that he loved me. I would take it if he would never leave. It was a balance, an inherent equilibrium. But now I saw this to be a falsehood, all of it. I withstood it because I chose to, and it had been for no reason at all.

I collected what little I thought of as valuable: personal documents, the few unbroken trinkets my parents had given me, the tea towels that had originally been in my mother's kitchen, some clothes, but not enough. I shut the windows, as if closing a holiday home for the long winter ahead. I carried everything, in one journey, to the car. Out front, the neighbours were mowing their lawns, hosing down their already spotless drives, calling to one another over their low fences. They turned to look at me as I unlocked the car. I nodded, a resolute, single movement, and they nodded back, with what I hoped was respect.

Eighteen

The first Friday in September, I asked Eddie to meet me at a bar after working hours, near where our old office had been. The town centre looked empty now, all abandoned shells, 'to let' signs, darkened glass. I got there ten minutes early, anxious I'd be late. I found a table outside, on the main street, and perched on the tall stool, feeling like I might slip off. The sun's heat channelled towards me, weaker now, and the smell of frying chips and vinegar wafted out the door of the bar and mixed with my perfume. I'd expected there to be more people around: couples clutching each other's hands, stalking to dinner; groups of women huddling together, slowly unwinding from work; teenagers playing loud music from their phones, unsure of what to do now summer had ended. They'd be realising it all didn't matter anymore. They were going to be someone else, soon.

I'd chosen somewhere neutral, nervous that Eddie would be angry and berate me in public – which I would have deserved. I didn't know what to expect from him, even though he had texted several times. His mum had made a full recovery, and I reassured myself that my actions had only indirectly caused the accident. But still, there was work to be done. Eddie's persistent messages had, as usual, finally made me decide to stop being a coward and talk to him in person.

I ordered a glass of lemonade, and, for Eddie, some odd-sounding pineapple-flavoured beer. I watched the bubbles race to the top of my glass, shoving past each other. With my boyfriend, apologising had been more straightforward. I didn't always know what I'd done wrong, but I'd have a sense of foreboding, and then he'd tell me. He was very clear in articulating my transgressions. It was apparent how I should apologise to him – on my knees. But with Eddie, the expectations weren't obvious. I didn't know how he'd want me to apologise.

Eddie ambled up the street, eventually, quite late but unapologetic. He was wearing a pair of dark sunglasses, so it was difficult to read his expression. Not angry, though, I thought. I wondered if he was late because he didn't want to come, and had been thinking of ways to get out of it. Perhaps he was already drunk, wanting to make the evening bearable.

'Thank you,' he said, picking up the beer bottle. He took a long drink. 'Not bad.'

'I thought it looked just disgusting enough that you'd like it,' I said, testing.

Eddie beamed, 'It's great.'

He began to tell me about how the last few weeks at work had been for him – how busy he'd been, how one of the new people in his team had almost caused a major data breach, which he'd discovered a moment before it was too late.

'And then, when I confronted him about it, he just started *crying*,' he said.

'He won't be coming back then,' I said.

'It's always the way with summer temps,' said Eddie. 'They never make it far into September.'

I felt sick, and knew I had to say something. I worried that the confrontation was imminent, but knew that it was unavoidable. I'd ran through the scenario several times on the journey here: Eddie, disgusted with me, threw his beer in my face; Eddie, appalled by my behaviour, shouted at me, called me a *cunt*; Eddie, offended by the sight of me, stood up and left without saying a word. In one scenario, I imagined he stood me up. Perhaps that might have been better.

'And your mum, is she okay?' I asked.

'The operation went fine, so she's back at home now. She's finally agreed to allow people into the house to help – but I don't know how long that will last.'

'You must have been really worried about her.'

'Yeah,' said Eddie, quietly. 'It was scary. But she's okay now, and I'm trying not to catastrophise and think about the future too much, or like, the what ifs.'

'I'm sorry I wasn't in touch more. I just didn't know what to say, but I should have texted or something.'

'That would have been nice.'

'Sorry. Is there anything I can do?'

'This,' he gestured to the table, 'is good.'

'Okay,' I said.

I tried to settle in a bit more, but spilled my lemonade onto my lap. I dabbed at my dress with a napkin. Someone from the bar brought out the bowl of chips I'd ordered:

golden yellow, steaming. The ketchup a perfect red. I ate one too quickly, eager for a distraction, and burned the roof of my mouth.

'How's the flat?' asked Eddie.

I chewed another chip, blowing on it intermittently. 'I think I'm finally settling in,' I said. 'No more fly infestations, at least. I don't know what happened. Honestly, I just think I'm cursed, but I'm trying to change my mind about that.'

Eddie took off his sunglasses now, and looked at me seriously: 'Are you okay?'

I decided to be honest. 'Yes and no. I shouldn't have called you about the flat, or when I was unwell,' I said.

'That was fine, honestly,' said Eddie.

'I've got to learn to look after myself. Or at least try.'

'Yeah, that's hard,' said Eddie. 'I think it's one of the hardest things to learn.'

I said, knowing I had to get this out, 'I appreciate everything you've done for me – the therapy appointment, driving me there, everything. You've been such a good friend to me. But I just don't think I could face counselling, not then.'

'It's okay,' he said. 'You've been a good friend to me too.'

I paused and smiled gratefully. Eddie smiled back.

I continued: 'It's not an excuse, but I was in a really bad relationship before I moved here. Sometimes, when I think about him – my ex-boyfriend – I worry it wasn't as bad as I think it was. I don't know if I escaped him because I was afraid, or if he'd actually broken up with me and I was too stupid to see it. So I think I've been behaving a bit erratically.'

'I'm so sorry,' said Eddie. He flinched, as if wanting to move, then realised he shouldn't.

'I suppose we both have to stop saying we're sorry at some point,' I said.

'Sorry,' Eddie laughed. 'So what *have* you been doing?'

'I told you I made friends with my next-door neighbour?' I said. 'Or maybe we've just been hanging out. But I think that's coming to an end now.'

'Well, some friendships are just meant to be for a certain time in your life,' said Eddie.

I wondered if he was trying to make a point about us. At times, he had an aphoristic way of talking that made him sound like one of Jess's inspirational quotes on Instagram. He had almost finished his beer now, and ordered another from a passing member of staff. A few other people, all in couples, dressed up for a long night out – heels and heavy make-up, short-sleeved shirts, strong aftershave – had sat down on the tables by us. They loudly ordered pitchers of cocktails, pints of beer, utterly happy, it seemed, absolutely without anything troubling them. The sun poured itself onto the back of my neck. I pressed my tongue to the burn on the roof of my mouth, and felt its fleshy pulse, the heat.

'Is that where all the witchy stuff was coming from, though? From your neighbour?'

I felt myself blush. 'Yeah,' I said. 'I'm not really sure the *witchy stuff* is for me.'

'Well, now you can try something else.'

'Like making kombucha?'

Eddie laughed, 'Yeah, maybe stick to the witchy stuff.'

'I think maybe I'll try therapy again,' I said, taking a mouthful of my drink. 'But properly this time.'

'I think it will be good for you,' said Eddie.

I stared at him and said, 'Do you think there's something really wrong with me?'

'Oh no, it's just that—'

'Because you shouldn't upset me,' I said. 'I can do terrible things.'

I laughed then, fully, and put my hand to my chest.

'I was joking, Eddie! That was a joke.'

'I just meant that therapy is good for everyone,' said Eddie.

'I don't think that's true.'

'Even so, it sounds like you're ready for it.'

Eddie and I went on drinking, talking. We ordered another bowl of chips, with peri peri salt this time. I felt safe in the golden sunbeams, enjoying the heaviness of my hands and arms, the looseness of my back, as I became tipsier. The waning heat made me want to lose my shoes and press my bare feet to the ground. The couples around us changed a few times, the outdoor area of the bar getting so loud we had to shout to hear each other. We talked about moving on to somewhere else, or going home, but ordered more drinks instead, until we were the only people left outside the bar.

On the walk home, the sky slowly turned to a lilac balm, and the trees murmured and sang. The last few bees crawled along the pavements, drifting to wherever they planned to go next. I left Eddie outside his flat with a quick but tight hug.

Nineteen

Several weeks later, I was due to leave the flat for one of my evening therapy appointments with Rob. I realised I'd not given him a fair chance. He was actually all right. It was already dark, and the moon cast a silvery gloss through the windows. On the street, the trees were turning into beacons, the lamp posts igniting the yellowing leaves. Some trees, still bushy, looked like plush fur coats. People walked up and down the pavement, their hoods up against the wind, hands stuffed into their pockets. The road itself was quiet – cars did not pull up, nor did they speed past with music blaring.

'Don't be late for your appointment,' my mum said.

I tucked my phone between my ear and shoulder while I pulled on my coat. 'I'll be fine,' I said, sniffling. My eyes felt heavy and sore, and my nose was burning with a cold, and from being rubbed vigorously with tissues.

'Do you think it's working?' she said. 'The therapy?'

'Well, it's not doing any harm,' I said.

'Will you text me when you're done?'

I promised her I would, as always.

It was true that the sessions were not causing me injury. Each time I returned to the flat after meeting Rob, the block was quiet, save for the reverberations of the clang of someone throwing their rubbish into the communal bins. Whatever tasks Rob had set me for the week seemed far away, even though I knew I would wake up the next day and feel determined; I would begin immediately. I was not enjoying the process, but I was, finally, starting to feel better, or more like my old self – the one who had existed *before* my ex-boyfriend. I caught flickers of her in mirrors, or in the shadowy reflections of car windows, and welcomed her back.

I shuffled through to the flat in my coat and boots, the sound of the coat's material like a breeze down the extractor fan. I knew the flat so well now that I could navigate it in the pitch-black, and sometimes tested myself with my eyes shut in the middle of the night. Water drummed from the tap into the sink. The smell of tobacco drifted upstairs. The new neighbours – the ones who had replaced Alice and Sean – must have been smoking again.

I flicked on the light in the kitchen, which had been slow to respond lately. It blinked like someone coming around from a deep sleep, then shone dimly – the bulb needed changing. I'd promised to meet Alice at her new house after my appointment, and stuffed a bottle of red wine into my bag.

Through the flat, I heard the front door crack open, its hinges groaning slightly, as though someone were leaning against it. I peered around the kitchen door, but, of course, no one was there. I took a step forward, and the front door swung open more widely, quietly this time, as though opening its arms.

And then I walked out into the night – not immediately better, or healed, or anything. But there I was.

Acknowledgements

Thank you to my agent, Matthew Turner, for making sure this book exists, and to his colleagues at Rogers, Coleridge & White. To my editors, Zoe Yang, Drew Weitman and Serena Arthur for patiently and perceptively shaping this novel. To Sareeta Domingo and Carina Bryan for welcoming me to Trapeze.

Thank you to my early readers and supporters, Ruth Gilligan and Luke Kennard. To my colleagues at Teesside University. Endless thanks to Miles Bradley, Jane Ford, Isabel Galleymore, Sasha Lindsey, Cynthia Miller, Elisha Owen, Nathaniel Spain and Millie Walker for listening to my plans, my doubts, and my concerns.

Thank you to my family – for everything, but especially for my love of nineties television programmes about the occult and the supernatural. To Jamie, for appearing as if by magic.

About the Author

Jenna Clake's debut collection of poetry, *Fortune Cookie*, won the Melita Hume Prize in 2016 and was published in 2017 by Eyewear. It received an Eric Gregory Award from the Society of Authors in 2018 and was shortlisted for a Somerset Maugham Award in the same year. Her poetry criticism has appeared in *Poetry London*, *The Poetry School*, and *The Poetry Review*. Her second collection, *Museum of Ice Cream*, was published by Bloodaxe and featured as one of *The Telegraph's* best new poetry books in 2021. She lectures in Creative Writing at Teesside University.

Disturbance is her first novel.